**Out of Burma**

By David Spiller

Copyright © 2013 by David Spiller

Also by David Spiller:

Pilot Error

Out of Burma

Great Singers of the 20th Century

Bridger's Diary – a Mozart fantasy

Girl at Dunkirk

(Available on Amazon)

# OUT OF BURMA

## ~ One ~

## Enter the Japanese

It began in Rangoon on 23rd December 1941. Jean Costain had returned home from the city centre with a decent-sized chicken (for Christmas day) and a new filling in her upper-left molar. Philip turned up soon afterwards, deciding that Jean's snacks were a better proposition than food from the 1st Glosters regimental mess.

He caught up with his wife in the kitchen. 'Did the Jap tooth bloke do a good job?'

'Impeccable.'

'I'm surprised he was tall enough to reach an upper molar.'

She gave an instruction to their Indian maid, Deepa, who was by the oven, and turned back to him. 'They say he's the best of the three Japanese dentists in town. But you know something – he's a nosey little devil. Kept asking me about you.'

'What do you mean?'

'Oh, about your job, how many men you were in charge of, whether you had to travel – stuff like that.'

'Crikey, Jean!' This was typical Philip-speak; he'd actually used the expression 'oh lor' a couple of days earlier. 'You didn't tell him, did you?'

'Well...I had to say something. It's not a secret, after all.'

He'd moved to stand a couple of paces away, still amiable, she thought, but the mood could quickly change. 'You do know,' he went on – and it was all right, because the tone was teasing – 'That the Japs bombed Singapore two weeks ago?'

'Of course I do.  Don't be ridiculous, Philip.  And everyone in Rangoon knows about the Glosters and the garrison.'

'I suppose.'  He took a bottle of beer from its crate and wrenched open the top.  'It's hopeless trying to keep tabs on Japs.  They're everywhere.  Dentists, photographers, masseurs...'

'Spies'

He grinned at her.  'They're pretty serious about Burma, be warned. You've heard the Jap slogan - "Asia for the Asiatics".'

Over lunch she started relaying some gossip picked up at the Pegu Club.  And then it happened.  She was never to forget the moment her life changed utterly.  Just as Deepa brought in the soup, Philip motioned his wife to silence and sat very still, listening.  Then she heard it too: a droning sound, low at first but growing in intensity.

'What is it?'

'I hardly dare think.'

He leapt up and bounded for the door.  She joined him on the front lawn, following his gaze at the sky over the city.  At first sight it resembled a single organism, like a giant space-ship.  Then she began to distinguish the individual aircraft.

'Bloody hell' came from Philip, who rarely swore.

'But surely...'  She could hear herself stammering.  'I mean, they're not going to...'

'Oh yes they are.'

As he spoke the first explosions came, and the first black smoke and sight of flames.  They stood hypnotised while the noise went on and on. Neighbours on the Prome Road came out of their houses to join them. Jean had covered her ears, and didn't realise it till she felt Deepa plucking at her sleeve.

'Sorry, madam.'

'What is it, Deepa?'

The Indian woman pointed at explosions on the horizon. 'Is it the dock place, madam?'

'What's that?' Jean was only half-listening, but then she remembered. Before she could speak, Philip broke into the conversation.

'Those are the docks all right. It's going to be sheer bloody murder down there.'

'*Philip*.' Jean tapped his arm and spoke quietly. 'Deepa's husband is a dock worker.'

'Oh, sorry.' He was off again, marching into the hall to lift the phone. She heard him curse and he flew back onto the lawn.

'Phone's bust. I've got to go in. You stay here, Jean. The city will be chaos.'

She hesitated. Her habit was to obey, but this was different. 'I must go in too. The hospital will need every nurse they can get.'

'Now look...'

'I have to, Philip. I can't just leave them to it.'

'All right, then.' He was always quick to a decision. 'I'll take you with me.'

'No – I'll have to get back again, and you won't know when. Besides, Deepa needs to get home. Public transport will be up the spout.'

He paused, and she knew he was thinking that the maid should make her own arrangements. With Deepa standing beside them he managed to restrain himself.

'I'll take the jeep,' she said to close the matter, and moved towards the house. 'Come on, Deepa.'

In the kitchen she faced her maid. The woman's usual demeanour — calm, almost haughty — had crumbled away; her hand trembled as she picked up some cutlery.

'Deepa, let's sit down and talk for a minute.'

'I'm all right, madam.'

'You're not all right.' Jean arranged two chairs at the kitchen table and almost dragged Deepa into one of them. Like the other servants, the maid would never sit in the memsahib's presence. 'Of course you're not. I'll get you some water.'

'I can get, madam.'

'I know you can, but let me do something for a change.'

She filled a glass from the contraption that was always kept supplied with boiled water, and sat still as Deepa drank. It was a way of not thinking, concentrating on this one thing: her maid's problems. All the other questions could wait. The kitchen was curiously quiet, although outside she heard Patrick charge off in his military vehicle, and then the remorseless clatter of bombs falling on the city.

'Who wouldn't be worried, Deepa?' she said. 'You'll feel better once you know what's happened. Now look, I'm going to drive to the hospital. Let's call at the docks on the way.'

'Thank you, madam.'

The maid seemed about to say more, then stopped.

'What is it?' Jean asked. 'Is there something else?'

'Sorry, I worried about Jyoti.'

'Jyoti?'

'Daughter, madam.'

'Of course.' Jean cursed herself silently. 'Jyoti, of course. I'm so sorry. Where is she?'

Deepa checked the clock on the wall. 'Now she is at home. Woman collect from school and take her home.'

'Then shall we go there first?'

Deepa hesitated. 'If madam can...'

Jean sprang to her feet. 'Madam *can*. Let's go.'

The maid looked round the kitchen at the dirty pots and pans, but Jean made a dismissive gesture. 'Good lord, don't bother about them. Come on.'

The jeep was old, but Jean had always felt comfortable in it. She drove with the hood up through an unfamiliar Rangoon, in which traffic of all kinds had been magically wiped from the streets. Deepa was in the passenger seat twisting her hands together. It was the first time she'd been in the vehicle.

'Jyoti must be – what? – nine years old now,' Jean said, seeking to distract with conversation.

''Eleven, madam.'

The shocking noise of aerial assault had stopped, and they passed nothing to indicate what had been going on – nothing except the place where a Jap pilot had bombed a field of cows. The animals lay peaceful and apparently unmarked around craters in the grass.

Following Deepa's instructions Jean drove through parts of Rangoon she'd not seen before, a far cry from the smart modern houses on her usual routes. She pulled up by a low shed-like construction with a corrugated iron roof.

The maid climbed from the Jeep. 'I will be quick madam.'

'It's all right, Deepa. Take as long as you need.'

Deepa disappeared under the corrugated roof and Jean stayed in the jeep. Surprisingly, her thoughts were not about the Japanese, though it seemed to have taken the Yellow Peril to bring about their disclosure. She was feeling distinctly uncomfortable – *guilty* was a better word – about her attitude to Deepa. The half-hour spent with the maid had sparked it off. Philip's dismissive attitude to the servants, entirely typical of his military colleagues, had embarrassed her on several occasions in the past, yet who was she to claim the high moral ground? It occurred to her only now that she'd taken minimal interest in a woman who worked for her six days a week. She'd no idea where Deepa lived, had forgotten the daughter's name and forgotten her age. Philip at least had the excuse of a demanding job; Jean's work was three half-days a week. And it was no use claiming that Deepa's detached manner discouraged intimacy, because Jean hadn't tried. Was she even a little bit jealous of her maid, she wondered. She at least had noticed, as Philip hadn't – because he looked through Indians as if they were ghosts – that Deepa was beautiful; beautiful in her upright bearing and proud expression and in every physical consideration.

She was so engrossed by these thoughts that Deepa had to tap on the windscreen to get her attention. The maid was outside beside a small girl with a solemn face. Jean got out of the jeep.

'Jyoti, madam.'

'Hello Jyoti. It's nice to meet you at last.' She wondered about shaking hands, but decided against. The girl gave a little nod, but nothing more. 'Does she speak English? Jean asked.

'Speaking better than me. Learning at school.'

'Well that's good. Is everything all right here?'

Deepa shook her head. 'Problem, madam. Woman who look after Jyoti, she go away. Leave Jyoti alone.'

'Oh no! She shouldn't have done that.' Into Jean's head came the slightest thought, no more, that this was a harbinger of future problems; that workers of all kinds would become unreliable or vanish from the face of the earth. 'What would you like to do?' she asked. 'Shall we take Jyoti with us?'

Deepa assented gratefully. Mother and daughter climbed into the jeep and they drove towards the docks area.

Jean had seen the docks only once before, when she and Philip arrived on a liner from Calcutta. Her recollection was of a huge area: extensive tracts of waterside and ships of many kinds plying the Rangoon river. She understood the need for a large facility. Burma's economy was almost entirely agricultural; everything else had to be imported. And apart from the new Burma Road – the one that led to China – there were no land communications with other countries; goods came into Rangoon by sea and were distributed by train or boat, in the latter case up-river on the Irrawaddy.

Sure enough as the jeep swept onto the waterfront the magnitude of the area surprised her all over again. But that was the least of it. There was a sharp intake of breath from Deepa as they got their first sight of damage inflicted. As far as the eye could see the wharfs were disfigured by bomb craters. Several big warehouses had been damaged and one was burning fiercely. Another had its doors wide open and an opened crate of champagne at the entrance. It was clear that looters had begun their work; more boxes were split apart and scattered about the wharf. Not far away two men were hacking at a wooden crate with an axe.

In the far distance a pall of black smoke announced more flames. They came from dozens of lorries lined up on the quay, several of which had sustained a hit. For a moment Jean wondered who could possibly have requisitioned so many vehicles, then remembered that Philip had said something about it. The Americans, seeking to bolster up China against the Japanese, had begun a massive programme of sending supplies. They called it 'lease-lend', or something similar. The lorries would be driven down the Burma Road into China.

Jyoti spoke to her mother in Hindi, pointing towards a paddle steamer that lurched at a drunken angle. It was far from the only ship in trouble. A slick of wreckage in the river suggested that one of the smaller craft had been sunk altogether.

Jean turned to look at the girl, wishing they hadn't brought her along. Far worse than the raid's effect on property was the human dimension. There was no disguising the dozen or so bodies scattered around the immediate area. A few had some sort of covering thrown over them, but most lay as they'd fallen. Elsewhere on the concrete quayside were dark pools that could only be blood, presumably from men wounded and taken off to hospital. Jyoti noticed all this and more – Jean felt sure of it – but the girl's dainty features betrayed no feelings one way or the other.

Jean's attention was drawn towards a spurt of movement on the wharf. Not far away a working party of Indian coolies was unloading a damaged vessel under the direction of a foreman – an Anglo-Burman, she guessed, from the characteristic, flattish features.

Deepa stiffened and pointed. 'That Indian man, I know. Friend of my husband.'

'Come on then.'

They left the jeep to approach the group, Deepa pressing Jyoti's face into her sari to shut out the carnage. As she talked to the Indian coolie, the foreman turned his attention to Jean.

'Bad, Mrs – very bad.'

'It's horrible,' she said. 'Were a lot of people hurt?'

'So many people.' He turned to bark an order at the coolies. 'Here on the wharfs and on the ships. Captain Ferns from the *Nepaul* – Mandalay steamer – he is killed. Many others, good men, dead. And these...' He nodded towards the Indian coolies, sneering. 'These people...also dying, like rats.'

Jean stared. It was well enough known that Burmans and Indians had their differences, but she'd never heard them put so explicitly.

'Why do you say "these people" in that way?' she asked.

The Burman spat into the river. 'People like that...they get what they deserve.'

Deepa interrupted at this moment. She *ran* towards them – a surprising sight given that she'd abandoned her normal stately manner of progress.

'Subhas hurt, madam. His friend see it happen. They take him to hospital.'

'Deepa, I'm sorry. We must hope it's not serious. Let's go and find him straight away.'

'He will be in the Indian hospital,' Deepa said.

'I don't think so.' The Burman had interrupted, highly animated. He actually chortled, an unpleasant braying sound quite unlike laughter. 'Obviously you have not heard. The Indian hospital has been bombed also. What a shame. There will be more dead Indians.'

Jean recoiled in disgust. She even wished Philip was with her. He'd have put the fear of god into the man; he did it on principle with all the 'natives', as he called them. She gave the foreman her own version of a withering glance. The bombing had obviously exaggerated old racial antipathies in a sickening manner. Everything had changed; she saw that now. Yet Deepa seemed unsurprised. The maid turned her haughtiest gaze upon the Burman with a gesture of courage and self-control more eloquent than words. For the first time Jean began to feel admiration for her spirited maid. And little Jyoti weighed in with a pint-sized imitation of her mother, standing erect and defiant beside her. In other circumstances it would have almost been comical.

She took Deepa's arm. 'Let's go.'

The scale of the tragedy got clearer as they moved towards the hospital building. The approach road, awash with desperate figures, had the medieval intensity of a Bosch painting. Events were clearly beyond the St John's Ambulance Brigade, who were were nominally responsible for Rangoon's casualty arrangements. Wounded men and women were making their own way to the hospital gates, some supported by friends, others stumbling unaided. Jean saw two people crawling there.

She parked the jeep and the three of them moved towards the main entrance. Again Jean felt sorry that Jyoti was there to witness the bloodshed. And she knew it would get worse once they were inside the building.

'When we get in I'll have to report to Matron,' she told Deepa. 'I'll ask her if I can leave Jyoti in the office. She won't see what's happening from there.'

'Much better, madam,' Deepa said, clearly relieved.

Then there would be the grim business of looking for Deepa's husband. Jean wasn't at all sure she would recognise the man; they'd only met once, and then briefly. The phrase 'All Indians look alike,' ran through her head. It was a constant refrain of Philip's fellow-officers.

'I'll look out for your husband,' she said, 'But it's best if you search for him yourself. Go from ward to ward and look at every patient.'

'Yes madam.'

'I'm afraid it won't be very nice.'

'I know, madam.'

She pushed through the hospital's swing doors into a scene of bedlam. In the entrance hall a handful of staff tried to deal with the people who had recently arrived. Most of the injured were grimly silent, but the hordes of relatives set up a wailing that reverberated round the stone walls. The hospital's facilities had been overwhelmed by the emergency. Equipment, in short supply at the best of times, was totally inadequate against the deluge of incomers. Jean saw one stretcher in use, but all except the worst cases had to move themselves along.

She hurried her two companions through the crowd and installed Jyoti in the office – making sure Deepa knew how to find her. Then she found Matron in ward 3.

'Nurse Costain, good,' the woman said. 'I can use you.'

No chance of a 'Thank you for coming in,' and Jean hadn't expected one.  Matron was a formidable character, tall, with short hair arranged round a severe expression.  She had odd Chinese-looking eyes, though her stature made Chinese blood unlikely.  Not that any of the nurses would have dared to ask about it – any more than they'd have enquired about an older husband rumoured to feature in Matron's past.  They knew little about their unnerving boss.  They were certainly ignorant of her Christian name; some of them found it hard to imagine she had one.

The woman told Jean to report to ward 5 and give what help she could to Dr Sheffield, the elderly British medic there.

'What about the injuries, Matron?' Jean asked.  'Are we talking about shock, shell fragments, that sort of thing?'

'In a lot of cases,' Matron replied.  'Obviously.  But many people have been machine-gunned.  The Japanese fighter pilots seem to enjoy that sort of thing.  I'm told hundreds were mown down in the park.  So you'll be getting bullets out.'

'Yes ma'am.'

'And nurse Costain,' she said as Jean made to leave.  'You must use your own judgement.  This is not a normal situation.  Do you understand?'

'I...I'm not sure.'

Matron stepped closer and lowered her voice.  'This hospital just about scrapes by in peacetime, nurse.  You must have noticed that.  In no sense are we equipped for a situation like this.  Normally, what a nurse can and can't do is tightly controlled, don't you agree?'

'Yes, Matron.'

'Today the rules have to be re-written.  Our doctors cannot possibly handle all these cases.'  She spoke even more quietly.  'Dr Sheffield  is struggling – *has* struggled for quite a while now.' Nothing highlighted the crisis more clearly than Matron disparaging a doctor to a nurse. 'I believe you are competent,' she went on. 'If you think you know what to do, then do it. You may save a life. Some of your decisions will be wrong, but you have my backing in any event. Now go and do your best.'

Before she could reach ward 5 Jean was intercepted by Deepa. The maid looked like a woman in shock, but still spoke levelly.

'Sorry madam. It is Subhas.'

'You've found him?'

Deepa nodded. 'It is bad. Please come.'

Deepa led the way, almost running. Jean told her 'Deepa, I have to do as I'm told here – but I'll look at him and see if I can help.'

Jean thought she'd prepared herself for the wards, but the first sight of one was a shock. Wounded men and women lay everywhere – in the beds, on trolleys and on the floor, in the corridor outside. Most beds had two bodies in them arranged head to toe. There had been no attempt to separate men from women.

'Here madam.'

Deepa's husband lay on the floor, on a plastic groundsheet spread against the wall. His head rested on a rumpled towel. There was blood all over his clothes.

'Let me see.' Jean knelt beside the man. It was a face typical of a certain kind of Indian, plump, with a small moustache, but transfigured by a terrible pallor. 'How do you feel, Subhas?' she asked.

'Pain, madam,' came in a whisper. The man was in shock and very frightened. 'Pain.'

'Let me see.'

She put both hands to his top-garment and ripped it open to the waist. Blood was seeping from two bullet holes in the right side of his chest. ('*Many people have been machine-gunned.*') Jean struggled to hide her expression, from the patient and from his wife. The impassive medical stare was harder to manage if you knew the person, even slightly. Looking at the man's injuries she couldn't imagine he would survive, even with the best medical attention – and he wouldn't be getting that.

'I'll see if we can help with the pain,' she told him.

Deepa was kneeling beside her, and she covered the maid's hand with her own. The gesture felt strange. 'Give me a moment,' she said.

Across the ward, orderlies were removing a body from one of the beds. They did it without ceremony, allowing the dead woman's head to loll down so that her long hair dragged along the floor. The second patient in that bed was unconscious, uncaring whether he lay next to a living person or a corpse.

A young nurse was working in the ward. Jean knew her slightly; they'd shared a pot of tea one evening in the hospital canteen. She went across and pointed to where Subhas lay on the floor.

'Susan, forgive me – I know that man. At least, he's married to my maid. If there's anything you can do...some morphine, or...' She stared meaningfully at the half-vacated bed. 'I'm sorry – I know I shouldn't.'

The nurse smiled wanly. 'Don't worry Jean – it's the way of the world. Leave it to me.'

As Jean left the ward, Subhas was being lifted into the spare bed-place. She felt relieved and at the same time uneasy. She thought:

We're not going to see much in the way of fairness during this calamity. People will grab any advantage to survive – and I'm one of them. Nationality, money, a friend in the right place; *it's the way of the world.*

That day Jean worked as she'd not worked before. Up to now her regular half-day stints at the hospital had been sedate affairs. She'd treated the victims of strokes and heart attacks and those recuperating from cancer surgery. The patients had been distressed, of course, but generally unsurprised by their circumstances. Injuries from violence were rare, save for the ones inflicted by *dahs* – the sharp knives fixed to wooden staves and used as weapons, a regrettable custom of the Burmese. Stitching up *dah* wounds in an emergency was as close as she'd come to blood. Her main duties had been about bed-pans, bandages, tea and sympathy.

And now this. Procedures that she'd occasionally seen executed by others now came before her with sickening regularity. She used hypodermic needles until they felt like extensions to her hand. She made up prescriptions formerly considered well beyond her competence. She inserted more stitches than the Indian tailors along Phayre Street. The thing she disliked most was probing for bullets, though that job had to be done too.

It surprised her that mental strain was more taxing than the physical exertion involved: checking her diagnoses, calculating complex prescriptions, saying the right things to patients. Above all – the power of life or death – deciding which patients to treat first. It was something that had to be learnt at double-quick speed. The first patient she approached had been a young woman with horrendous burns across her torso. Jean knew this meant a laborious task of picking off the dead skin with tweezers. She didn't have the time and there was no-one else to do it. She told an orderly which pain-killers to administer and moved on. The next patient had half the flesh on his chest shorn away, internal organs exposed. Here something could be done immediately. She inserted gauze, vaseline and sulphanilamide and gave the man some reassuring words. She didn't expect either patient to live through the night.

Matron looked in several times, and at 7pm came to the ward and told her 'Go home'.

'It's all right, Matron,' she said. 'I can carry on.'

'Don't you know when you're beat, girl. Go home now, or you'll be no use to me tomorrow.'

She found Deepa waiting in the office with Jyoti. Unusually – Deepa's appearance was always impeccable – the maid's sari was stained and creased. It turned out that she'd gone round her husband's ward with a mop, then got down on her knees and scrubbed every vestige of blood off the floor.

'I'm sorry you've had to wait so long,' she said.

'No problem, madam.'

Jean turned to the daughter. 'And you, Jyoti. You've had a very long wait. Were you very bored?'

The girl was expressionless. 'No madam.'

'Come on. I'll take you both home.'

Jean saw little traffic on the roads, but a disturbing new feature was apparent as she turned the jeep towards Deepa's suburb. She passed a wooden shack in flames, a conflagration that seemed all the more vivid in the darkened streets. A boisterous crowd of onlookers was at the roadside, and as Jean drove past someone pointlessly hurled a rock into the bonfire, smashing a window. A bit further on someone else's home was burning brightly. And near Deepa's house yet more places were alight, amidst an atmosphere of fevered excitement in the street. She stopped the jeep and killed the engine.

'All these fires. What's going on, Deepa?'

'Indian homes, madam.'

'But...why? Who's doing this?'

The maid was silent. 'Deepa?' Jean pressed.

'Burmans, madam.'

Jean put a hand helplessly to her forehead. Little by little the scales were falling from her eyes on this horrible day. 'I've been thinking,' she said, 'That you'll find it hard getting to the hospital. Who knows what the buses will be like. And now...with all this going on. Will you be safe here without your husband there?' Again Deepa was silent. 'What I've been thinking,' Jean went on, 'Is that you and Jyoti could stay at our house. There's a spare room – you know, the one that looks onto the back garden. I can drive you about.' She stared at the maid, willing her to answer. Flames from the burning house two doors along cast lurid patterns onto Deepa's face. 'To be perfectly honest,' Jean said, 'It would help me to have you around.'

Eventually the maid spoke. 'Thank you, madam.'

'Is that a "yes", Deepa?'

'Thank you, madam.'

'All right then. You and Jyoti go in and get together everything you'll need. Call me when you're ready.'

Deepa took remarkably few things from her shack – perhaps because she had few things to take, Jean reflected – and within 20 minutes they were back on the road.  Still the day's surprises were not over.  Jean's bungalow was on the Prome Road, the highway that ran more or less alongside the rail line to the town of Prome, 120 miles to the north.  Normally the road saw little traffic after dark; indeed little movement of any kind, save for the bands of pi dogs scavenging for food.  This evening as Jean turned into the home stretch she found Prome Road congested with traffic: *human* traffic – men, women and children of all ages, many pulling handcarts piled with possessions, other carrying loads on their shoulders, hundreds of them plodding north in a silent procession.  She had to edge the jeep down the road alongside the flood of humanity.

Jean was utterly taken aback.  'What on earth...' she spluttered. 'What's going on, Deepa?  What are these people doing?'

'Indians, madam.  Leaving.'

'Leaving?'

'Leaving Rangoon.'

'But...'  Jean sounded the hooter at a knot of handcarts that had spilled across both sides of the highway.  'I don't understand.  Where on earth are they going?'

'India, madam.'

'India?  *India*!  But they can't be.  It's a thousand miles.  There are no roads out.  They'd never make it.  Surely...'

'India, madam.'

I'll ask Philip, Jean thought to herself, dismissing the maid's assertion as ludicrous.  She could never have dreamt that the conversation would be relevant to her own circumstances within the next two months.

Arriving home, she manoeuvred the Jeep through the file of Indians and into her driveway. The bungalow was in darkness. As Jean climbed from the Jeep an unlooked-for sensation of faintness came over her. Her knees buckled. She thought she'd fall and stopped to rest her head on the bonnet. Sounds of the doleful procession were still audible from the road behind her.

Deepa materialised at her side. 'Madam.'

'It's all right, Deepa. I'm just being silly. What on earth's the matter with me?'

'Too much work. Madam working hard all day.'

'It's just one afternoon,' she said, angry with herself. 'You work harder than that every day.'

'Different, madam.'

It's different all right, she thought. Deepa was used to hard work; she wasn't. A single day...the biggest learning experience of her life. And it was only beginning. She'd once overheard an Anglo-Burman, a rifleman, refer to English military wives as 'plucky little women'. She'd been furious at the time.

'Right,' she said firmly. 'Let's get your things inside. No, Deepa, I know...but I'm *going* to help you.'

Once they'd installed Deepa in the back room Jean's aspirations towards self-sufficiency evaporated. She found herself in an armchair, double gin in hand; then in the bath for which Deepa had heated up water. The ability to think seemed to have deserted her. It was hard enough to concentrate when – in the kitchen, eating Deepa-prepared tinned sausages and rice (for there was no escaping rice in Burma) – the maid said 'Subhas, madam, he is very bad'.

It was a statement rather than a question. 'He *is* bad,' she said. 'I'm sorry, Deepa. But he's alive and we must hope. I will go to see him every day.'

'Good night madam,' Deepa said, quietly leaving the room.

Philip got in around ten. He was done in, and his mood didn't improve when he found Deepa installed in the spare room. He softened when the maid prepared hot water for him to bathe, and again when she rustled up some food in the kitchen.

'I had no choice, Philip,' Jean said, keeping him company while he ate. And it's going to be very helpful having Deepa here.'

'We'll see how it goes,' was all he would say.

She asked about his day. 'Seems like it's going to be a while before I can shoot at Japs,' he told her.

'I'm very glad to hear it. If you can shoot at them, they can shoot at you.'

He smiled. 'I *am* in the army, Jean. Shooting's part of it. No, from now on I'm in charge of keeping order. Keeping Rangoon operational. We were out in the stores this afternoon, hunting looters.'

She told him about the looting she'd seen in the docks. Then she remembered the horrible way the Burman foreman had spoken about Indians, and told him that too.

'Are you surprised?' he said.

She thought about it. 'I am a bit. All right, I don't really know any Burmans' – and have never invited any to my home, she thought – 'But when I deal with them in the bazaars they seem quite fun...easy-going.'

'But then you're spending money with them, aren't you?'

'I suppose that's it.'

'Yes, my sweet.'

It struck her as strange, sitting together in the kitchen at such a late hour. Everything was out of kilter, yet despite the dreadful day – and the dreadful future, in all probability – the mood between them was unusually relaxed. The power supply had not been restored and the room looked almost romantic swathed in shadows cast by candles.

'Burmans aren't as cuddly as you think,' Philip said, lighting a cigar. 'Yes, they're easy-going – "lazy" might be a better word. But they're unreliable. I wouldn't give tuppence for the ones we have in the regiment if it comes to fighting. Much rather have Chinns or Karens. The Burmans'll be up and away to join the freedom movement.'

'Why do they dislike Indians so much?'

'It's complicated. They look down on them because Indians do all the menial jobs, but then they rely on them to keep things running. And they're deeply resentful of the Indian money-lenders.' He shook his head. 'I really don't know, Jean. You have to remember the Burmese *hated* being regarded as part of India. They've only been independent for five years – well, we're supposed to be ultimately in charge, of course.'

He drew deeply on his cigar. Jean sipped a cup of tea and slapped at a mosquito that had penetrated the bungalow's defences. From the road came the muted sound of Indians trudging on in the darkness. She gestured in their direction.

'Philip, I asked Deepa about the people out there. She says they're making for India. *India*. Can that really be true?'

'I admit it's a surprise, this exodus,' he said. 'A real surprise. I'm sure the brass didn't expect it. I suppose some of these people will have relatives in Upper Burma, but the rest...well when you think about it, where else could they be going?'

'I still don't believe it. *One* air raid...'

'That killed two thousand people.'

'Oh! As many as that?'

'That's the first estimate. Look, the Indians have been uneasy since thirty-seven, when Burma broke free. They function all right here as long as they're under our protection. If we were to leave  the Burmans would give them hell, and they know it. So when you think about it' – he got up from the table – 'This migration doesn't say much for their confidence in us, does it?' He yawned. 'Time for bed, eh?'

Upstairs in the big double bed their mood of intimacy soon melted away. Despite the excitements of the day – or perhaps because of them – Philip wanted sex. The unimaginative, almost military way he went about this invariably irritated her. It was the same routine every time: he'd reach across the bed to put a hand on her right breast – always the right one – as if this activated some sort of power switch. Sex was the last thing on Jean's mind and she tried to deflect him with more questions.

'Will there be more raids, Philip?  Do you think the Japanese could drive us out?'

He didn't answer at first and she thought he was sulking. 'War in the far east is unlikely at present,' he said eventually. 'That's the Whitehall view.'

'But...'

'Of course, they don't know what they're talking about.'

'But could the Japanese...you know, win?'

'They've got three airfields nearby to attack us from, so that's a good start. But hey, everything's all right. If there's an invasion, the Burmese will rise up and fight. The Governor himself has announced it.'

'You don't think so?'

'I'm just an intelligence officer. No use asking me.' He fell silent again and she thought the conversation was over. Then: 'Wavell was here a couple of days ago. He was appalled at what he found...how unprepared we are.'

'Who's Wavell?'

'Oh for god's sake, Jean.' He was up on one arm now, anger fuelled by weariness and frustration. 'Try and keep up, can't you.'

'I might if you ever lowered yourself to tell me things,' she rapped back with unaccustomed sharpness.

He sighed theatrically. 'Wavell's about to become the Commander-in-Chief in India. He'll decide what happens here, god help us.'

'So...you say he was appalled. *Why*? Talk to me, Philip. Imagine I'm an intelligent human being. What did he find that so appalled him?'

He levered himself up and wedged the pillow behind his back, apparently ready to talk. 'You know Sergeant Johnson, don't you?'

'Well?' she said, sitting up in her turn. 'What about it?'

'What do you think of him?'

'I like him.' She visualised Johnson's substantial figure seated in the mess with a pint glass of beer in hand. 'He's like a favourite uncle.'

'Precisely. Can you imagine Johnson in the jungle charging at a Jap company with fixed bayonet – ripping someone's guts out, kicking their teeth in.'

Jean giggled. She couldn't help it; the image was so preposterous.

'It's not funny, Jean. That's what we're up against. The Japs have a jungle warfare school in Formosa. They're experts. We don't have a clue. Johnson couldn't *find* the jungle if you showed him on a map. He joined the Glosters for the drink – and the women.'

'I'm lost here,' Jean admitted. 'Do the other officers think like you?'

'They don't think – that's the trouble. What do you imagine we have in Burma by way of fighting troops?' Before she could comment he answered his own question. 'A couple of brigades up north. You saw something of them when you made that trip to Mandalay. A few other odds and sods, including the Gurkhas, thank god. And that's it.' She thought: he's relieved to be spelling this out, even if it's only to me; things he couldn't repeat to senior officers. 'We hold Burma by bluff, Jean,' he went on. 'A few formations in a few places, with little trust between them. Most Burmese have never seen a British soldier. No, if the Japs want this country – and god only knows why they would – they'll take it.'

He had the wind in his sails now; she'd asked for it, and she was getting it. 'We're in no shape to fight – no shape at all,' he went on. 'We're well below strength anyway and the men are prone to malaria. The officer cadre's been milked for other units from India to Timbuktu. Some officers don't know their men. And they don't know their language. My Urdu's above the norm and it's not up to much, as you know very well.'

He paused for breath, then resumed as if someone had wound him up. 'We've no mortars to speak of. Better artillery than the Japs but not enough of it. We're desperately short of vehicles, even of mules – though there's an arsenal of horse-shoes. There aren't enough wireless sets – we rely on local communications and the enemy are bombing them.  And that's not the worst of it, if you really want to know.  Very soon now the Japs will be in complete control of the air, and then it's going to be sheer bloody carnage.'  He thumped furiously at the pillows. 'There you are, Jean, I hope that puts your mind at rest.  And now if you don't mind I'm going to sleep.'

## ~ Two ~

## Christmas day bombing

On Christmas day morning Jean rose at 7am, leaving Philip in bed. She found Deepa in the kitchen preparing chicken for an early lunch. (It was all but impossible to get up earlier than Deepa.) She went onto the veranda with a cup of tea and sat in a wicker chair gazing at the garden. In the early sunlight the marigolds, hollyhocks and dahlias clustered around the lawn were ridiculously colourful. How long will this scene remain presentable, she wondered, now the gardener has gone missing. Let it be a few weeks at least. The peaceful routine of sitting out first thing was important to her. She might even have forgotten about bombing raids were it not for the Indian walk-out on the road beyond the garden wall – sparser than it had been but still substantial.

After the first ferocious raid there'd been no more sightings of Japanese aircraft, and a tenuous optimism had settled on Rangoon's residents. 'Perhaps those yellow devils were just demonstrating what they can do,' was the view of her next door neighbour on the Prome Road. As usual Philip was more circumspect. 'They'll be working out a strategy,' he told her. 'If the blighters ever manage to take Rangoon – god forbid – they'd want to have the key installations intact. Bombing the docks was a crazy thing to do.'

Matron had asked Jean to take an early Christmas lunch and start work at one, to which she'd readily agreed. She felt surprisingly OK that morning, after the two hardest working days of her life. Arms and shoulders were stiff from bending over beds, but her head was clear and she felt ready for more action. In a guilty sort of way she'd almost relished the experience. 'I've actually been of use to other people,' she told herself. 'Maybe I'm not the disaster area Philip thinks I am.'

The day before, she'd done a little evening shopping in the wealthy trading areas of Oliphant Street. Some shops and bazaars had been closed but a little business was done early and late in the day, when traders felt more secure from the bombers. What nobody could fail to notice was how – in just two days – prices had gone through the roof.

Jean became aware that Deepa was standing beside her. The maid had an extraordinary facility for moving silently with no diminution in elegance.

'Good morning, Deepa.'

'Good morning, madam.'

'Still people are leaving.' Jean indicated the road. 'When will it stop?'

'Maybe not stop,' Deepa said. 'Everything depending on that.' She pointed at the sky. 'If Japanese coming, Indians leave. Indian people with money, many left before – boats to Chittagong or Calcutta.'

'A boat would be a lot easier than walking.'

Deepa hesitated, clearly with information to impart; it was amazing how the jungle network spread its rumours through local communities. I should be better informed than I am, Jean thought, married to an intelligence officer and with Deepa as a maid.

'Easier than road, but dangerous also,' Deepa said. 'Bad time for

Indians on the boats. Hearing bad stories too many people. Japanese attack boats also. Not all good, madam.'

Encouraged by what was in Deepa terms a positive flood of information, Jean asked another question. 'What about you, Deepa? What are your plans?'

'Waiting for Subhas to get better. Waiting and hoping.'

'Of course.'

'Hoping to stay working for madam.'

'You can work for us as long as you like, you know that. And stay here at the house of course.'

'Thank you, madam.'

Privately Jean thought Subhas hadn't a chance, but she could hardly press Deepa on that. They'd have to wait and see.

When she'd put it off as long as she could Jean went inside to sort out the toilet. She'd half-hoped Philip might tackle it, but he was oblivious to problems affecting the house. Burmese arrangements for bodily functions were still medieval. Bungalows along the Prome Road were regarded as novelties by most locals – places where the owners put pictures onto the walls and entertained their guests on chairs. But old-style bucket toilets were still the norm and had to be emptied – and the 'outside sweeper' in their overstaffed household was another who'd not turned up to work. Jean dragged the foul-smelling bucket from its resting place and lugged it towards the pit behind the building. Deepa hurried to help but Jean told her 'Better not mix up this job with the cooking'. As she went through the back door the over-full container slopped over onto her foot. She thought: how tenuous the distance is between my privileged existence and real life as endured by most of the population.

Shortly afterwards she came across Jyoti. The girl stayed in her room for much of the time, but here she was at the kitchen table as her mother worked. She sat very upright – in Deepa style – reading a children's book in English.

'Hello Jyoti.' Jean felt she should make an effort. 'Is everything all right?'

'Thank you, madam.' (Another echo of her mother.)

She cast around for something they could talk about. 'It's Christmas day. Do you know about Christmas?'

'My teacher told us something,' Jyoti said. 'There was a man called Jesus and he was born on this day.' Her unadorned style of speech might have been someone reading from the bible. 'Is Jesus your god, madam?'

Deepa was ready to interrupt but Jean held up a hand. 'Not really,' she said, having inherited godlessness from her father. 'I don't really have one. What about you? Do you have a special god?'

'I like Ganesh.'

'Ganesh! What is Ganesh?'

'Half of Ganesh is like me and half is like an elephant.'

'Goodness! That sounds very unusual.'

'Yes, madam.'

With that Jyoti returned to her reading. Well, the exchange at least resembled a conversation, Jean thought – one in which Jyoti had taught her something new. It was a start of sorts. The girl's manner suggested extreme detachment, a humouring of the memsahib because she was the memsahib. There'd been none of the standard child reactions to adults: boredom, cheekiness, resignation, trepidation, even a glimmer of interest. All perfectly understandable in the circumstances. Jean resolved to track down a picture of Ganesh in their home encyclopaedia.

Christmas lunch in the tropics was a strange experience, doubly so when taken at eleven in the morning. They made the best of it. Philip had found a box of crackers in an expatriate store, and they solemnly pulled one each. Jean's cracker joke ran: 'Why can you never be hungry in the desert? Answer: Because of all the sandwiches in it.' The home-made Christmas pudding lay heavily on their stomachs in the warm weather.

Afterwards she set out for the hospital. Deepa had turned down the offer of a lift, not wanting to expose Jyoti again to the hospital's traumas. An Indian neighbour had offered to look after the girl from 3pm – a promising development – and Jean pressed taxi fares upon Deepa for a later visit to town.

Jean took the jeep in through Rangoon's neatly laid out streets. Despite a partial return of the traffic, driving was a lot easier than usual. She was nearing the centre when an unfamiliar noise reached her ears: a kind of high-pitched wailing with no apparent source. Not until she noticed one wall of a house disintegrate in a hail of flying bricks did Jean identify the sound. It was an air-raid warning; the first one in Rangoon's history.

She pulled the jeep in to the kerb and ran from it towards a row of small trees at the roadside. Some people were there already, taking advantage of the minimal protection offered. All eyes were lifted upwards. Now she could see the sky Jean was astonished she'd not become aware of the raid earlier. There must have been two dozen twin-engined bombers cruising above, releasing their cargo upon the city. She'd not actually seen bombs fall before. Later on her description of them was 'small but noisy'. The sound reminded her of fire-crackers on Guy Fawkes day, though these crackers brought destruction in their wake. Standing absurdly vulnerable at the roadside she was anxious about the jeep, but a lot more anxious on her own account. Two Burmese women nearby had buried their faces on each other's shoulders, but Jean couldn't restrain herself from watching. She saw a telegraph pole topple across the road in stately but inexorable motion, and the live cables sparking on the asphalt surface. Further away (fortunately) a burst main gushed water onto the street.

As Jean looked on there was a thudding sound but no explosion, and a knot of people on the far side of the road scattered in panic.

'A dud,' announced an elderly Anglo-Burman standing next to her.

'What?'

'That was a bomb, but it didn't go off. Those people were lucky.'

'We've all been lucky – so far,' Jean said.

Now the steady progress of the bombers was interrupted as other aircraft came onto the scene, and machine-guns supplemented the fire-cracker noise. A ragged cheer issued from the onlookers as dog-fights began in the sky above.

'It's the Royal Air Force fighting back,' Jean cried in a fit of patriotic fervour.

'I'm afraid not, madam.' The Anglo-Burman seemed particularly well informed. 'These are the Tigers.'

'Tigers?'

'The Flying Tigers. Americans. American pilots out to have some fun.'

As he spoke, one of the Japanese bombers belched black smoke from its tail and dropped towards the city out of control. There was more cheering. A couple of parachutes came from the stricken plane but failed to open, and the men attached to them plunged to their deaths. This sparked a standing ovation from under the trees, and a group of sweet-looking Burmese girls jumped up and down waving parasols over their heads.

'Good riddance,' said the Anglo-Burman, turning on his heel to walk away.

Even after the bombers had left the scene a good ten minutes passed before Jean plucked up courage to follow the Burman's example. She stood staring at the devastation around her. The flat Rangoon landscape ensured that scenes of havoc were visible to quite a distance away. Curiously, the celebrated Shwe Dagon pagoda, visible on its hillside from any point in the city, seemed to have survived unscathed.

Rangoon was too big and spread out to be lovable, but it had aspects Jean was fond of and she wondered if they'd ever be the same again. She'd always enjoyed watching groups of young women shop in the bazaars, with their carefree manner and giggling conversations. With slim hips encased in colourful longyis and dainty feet in sandals, white-painted faces, and jewellery, and coiled hair decked with flowers (but not too many, or they'd be regarded as 'loose women'), the girls flitted about like humming birds in a cage. And after this carnage? Could they revisit the sprightly innocence of the world they'd always known? It seemed unlikely.

By good fortune the jeep was undamaged. Jean manoeuvred it round the fallen telegraph pole and followed an alternative route to work through the detritus of the bombing raid. The saddest thing she saw was a devastated temple, with five ravaged Buddhas side by side amidst a wreckage of charcoaled spars and sheets of corrugated iron; the most horrible, a pi-dog tearing at the flesh of a corpse in the gutter.

The hospital had secured an armed guard to watch over parked staff vehicles. As Jean stepped from the jeep the man shouted a warning. She jumped back just as a large animal galloped past rasping its rump against her shoulder. It charged round a corner, but not before she saw the black-and-white stripes that could only have signified a zebra.

'Nurse Costain – we were worried about you,' said Matron when Jean found her in the office.

Jean told her about the zebra. 'It's from the zoo,' the woman said. 'They've shot the dangerous animals and turned the others onto the streets. That's the least of it. The lunatics are out of the asylum and some fool has released the prison population. So watch your step out there.'

The 'second wave' of bomb casualties was coming through the hospital doors, though in significantly smaller numbers than the first. Even so the influx would have defeated their resources had not hundreds from the first tranche already been despatched to the mortuary. Jean worked furiously on the newcomers for six hours and was all but spent when she left the building at seven.

It was dark in the parking area and the guard had disappeared. She got into her jeep and started the engine. A wild cry came from near at hand and in the rear view mirror Jean saw a man's head and shoulders rise from the back seat. She swung round, heart thumping furiously.

'Who the hell are you?'

The intruder just sat there. His silence and stillness increased the sense of menace. It was so quiet that Jean could hear her own erratic breathing. For a second or two the headlights of a passing vehicle illuminated the man's staring eyes. She would have screamed had he not opened the rear door and slipped out. She saw his dim outline lurch slowly away.

Arriving home, the last thing Jean wanted was to go out again, but Philip had other ideas. He'd changed out of uniform and into some smart clothes. 'It's Christmas, darling,' he kept saying. He assured her she'd feel better after a bath, and indeed Deepa had already heated the water. She remonstrated and pleaded, to no avail. They were going out.

'If we must,' she told him, 'Let's do the Silver Grill. Red's Orchestra should be playing.'

Philip shook his head. 'Two of the fellows were there last night. The cook's still around, but the other staff have decamped *en masse*. The diners had to run about serving themselves. And they had nobody to do the washing up. Dirty plates all over the restaurant, apparently.'

'Well where, then?'

'We're meeting at the Minto Mansions.'

'The hotel? Oh Philip – it's so gloomy.'

'Yes *but*...they've still got most of their staff. Too old to join the exodus, it seems.'

'Exactly. I rest my case.'

'You'll be OK. It's the usual crowd. And some of the American pilots are coming.'

'The Tigers?'

He raised his eyebrows in mild surprise. 'Yes darling, quite right – the Tigers.'

Her spirits were scarcely raised when they passed through the hotel's cavernous reception area. The desk clerk's appearance reinforced Philip's observation about staffing; a wizened old Indian was propped up against the counter, deaf to all but the loudest attempts at conversation.

Near the entrance, mounds of trunks and suitcases were piled to a height above Jean's head. She sneaked a look at some labels – Mr S Biswas, Fairlawns Hotel, Calcutta; Mr R Majumdar, Park Hotel, Chittagong. These were some of the wealthy Indians Deepa had described as fleeing the country.

Philip's party were seated round one long table in the restaurant. They'd just been served with soup – an etiolated substance of no known provenance – when the wailing of air raid sirens sounded for the second time that day. All lights were doused and waiters hurried guests into the garden, where some slit trenches had been dug in the lawn. In the all but pitch-darkness Jean got separated from her husband, sharing a trench instead with one of the American pilots, a large fellow garishly dressed like his compatriots – in his case with a ten-gallon sombrero on his head.

'Don't you think that hat might attract the bombers,' Jean said by way of introduction.

The American considered this. 'You may have a point, lady, but on the credit side it'll offer protection against explosives.' He extended a meaty hand. 'I'm Mike.'

'Jean,' she said, as her own hand was engulfed by his. 'And you're one of the Flying Tigers?'

'I have that honour. The American Volunteer Group, to use our full title.'

'I saw you in action today. At least, somebody said it was the Tigers.'

'Wouldn't have been any other buggers. The British air support's a joke. You've got 16 ancient Buffalos — and that's it.'

'I saw a Japanese bomber go down.'

'Did you. Actually, today's score was 23.'

'Goodness! That's pretty good, isn't it?'

'We did all right.'

'And did you...you know, lose any yourselves?'

'We lost three.'

'Oh!'

She didn't know how to respond. The man had lost three colleagues that afternoon — friends, in all probability — and here he was a few hours later having a meal out. She'd not got the measure of war and the curious, heightened form of existence led by its protagonists.

'It's all right,' he said, sensing her embarrassment. 'We like what we do.'

She told him about the Burman who'd stood near her under the trees. 'He said the Tigers were out to have some fun.'

'We get paid as well, you know. The Chinks provide our wages — plus a bonus for every kill. They're not too fond of the Japanese.'

'No. So...would you say the Chinese are on our side?'

He turned his head to look at her. 'You know, that's a very good question.'

The air raid siren stopped abruptly, leaving the garden shockingly quiet. She found it a strange experience being crammed into a slit trench with the bulky American. There was no light beyond what came from a luminous moon; enough to show up the large bats that coasted in the sky above them. A murmur of voices came from other trenches. The scent of jasmine was everywhere.

'Should we climb out?' she suggested.

'Give it a bit longer.' He manoeuvred his body awkwardly in the narrow space. 'Can't hear any planes though. These siren jokers managed to miss the first raid altogether. Got this afternoon's, but now they've signalled a raid that isn't. Good all round performance, eh?'

'You're not impressed?'

'Now don't encourage me to use foul language, Jean. The Rangoon Corporation? They've not the slightest interest in civil defence. Useless at ARP. Uselessly late with shelters – they've got a few up now, but the cement's still wet. A lot of the people who were killed could have survived, you know, if the shelters had been ready. As for the fire service...half the engines wouldn't start but it didn't matter because the drivers had run away. You'd think with all these wooden buildings around...'

He stopped mid-rant as Jean started laughing.

'What?'

'All these complaints. It's like listening to my husband.'

'Is he the scratchy fellow with the little moustache.'

'Um...'

'Hey, I'm sorry. You must understand I'm from Texas. That's not an excuse – it's an explanation.'

She grinned. 'It's all right. Philip *is* scratchy.'

'Come on then.' He bounded from the trench with a large man's lightness of foot and heaved her out after him. 'Hope you like cold soup.'

The lights came back and they all returned to the table. They had reheated soup, then some scrawny bits of chicken – and rice, of course. Jean sat next to one of Philip's fellow-officers, who told a series of risqué jokes, including one about a chorus girl and a giant caterpillar. Her 20 minutes in the trench turned out to be the best bit of the evening.

Philip drove home savagely through empty streets. Their pre-dinner moods appeared to have been reversed. In his case the strains of the day had kicked in. He was deflated by the damp-squib evening and even seemed resentful that Jean had been closeted in a trench with the pilot. Jean, on the other hand, had rallied slightly; she was in irreverent mood, ready to poke fun.

As they racketed along she marvelled that a city could be so utterly transformed in two days. It was before midnight, yet the only signs of movement came from pi-dogs and the occasional figure shrinking away from the jeep's headlights. They could almost have dispensed with lights. Every couple of minutes lurid patterns danced on the windscreen as the jeep passed another bonfire; another home burning brightly with nobody in attendance.

'What *are* all these fires?' she said. 'Who's causing them? Why is nobody trying to put them out?'

'How the hell should I know,' Philip threw back at her, taking a bend with a screech of tyres.

'Oh I'm *so* sorry – I thought you would.' She was in a rare mood to needle him. 'I thought you were responsible for keeping order.'

'This is Burma, Jean. It's about time you twigged. This is Burmans burning the homes of Indians because they hate them. It's Burmans sacking the houses of the rich from envy. You don't like it? This is just the beginning.'

'Thank you so much, Philip,' she said, in a voice designed to cause maximum irritation; sometimes she couldn't help herself.

They went the rest of the way in silence. She half expected their own place to be in flames, but for some reason Prome Road had escaped the wave of ritual burnings.

There was no companionable cup of coffee together that evening. Deepa had retired for the night and Jean quickly followed suit. She lay alone in the double bed hearing the unnerving chorus of the pi-dogs. But she soon sat up when another sound came through the open window. Someone was moving about outside. If it was Philip, she hoped he'd taken a torch; the occasional snake still turned up on the Prome Road properties.

She slipped out of bed and drew back the curtain. Through the mosquito netting the face of a man looked in on her. She was struck by the odd expression in the eyes, not unlike that of the intruder in her jeep. The stranger showed no reaction as her own face came into his field of vision. He stood there in the darkness. She didn't feel scared this time. It may have been a different man but she felt she knew him, and knew he was safe. He inhabited a far stranger world than hers – though all their worlds were crazy now.

The bedroom door opened and Philip came in. 'What are you doing?'

he said.

'There's someone outside. It's nothing.'

He strode to the window. 'Jesus, you call that nothing. Don't you know this city is crawling with looters and convicts?'

'He's harmless, Philip. Leave him.'

He stuck his face against the mosquito netting and bellowed. 'You — get out of here *now*. If you don't you'll be sorry.'

The intruder stared. 'He's sorry already,' she said. 'Can't you see.'

'By god, I'm not having this.' Philip stamped back across the room. To Jean's alarm he went to  the tallboy and opened the top drawer. She knew what it contained: his Walther pistol.

'No, Philip, *no*.'

He went furiously from the room, pistol in hand, out of the front door and round the corner of the bungalow, Jean trailing behind in her night dress, barefoot, yelling.

It was dark down the side of the building but the intruder's wafery figure was half-illuminated by light from the window. Philip raised his pistol, shouting in an unrecognisable voice. 'I'll say this once more. *Get out...now*.'

Another voice Jean didn't know — her own — was making ridiculous, squeaky pleading sounds, because she knew what would happen. The stranger lurched forward and her husband fired. The man buckled at the knees and fell face down. The explosion reverberated round the garden to the wail of pi-dogs and Jean's screams. She threw herself down beside the body.

Philip was beside himself. 'What the hell are you doing?'

'I'm taking him to the hospital.'

'No you're not.'

As it happened, he was right. There was no response from the wretched man's pulse. All that remained was for Philip to drag the body off his property and down to the roadside. Any crime was permissible now, Jean realised, still on the ground with the soil rough against her bare knees. She cried bitterly, less for the doomed man who lay in the Prome Road gutter than for herself; for something she thought she had that was now ebbing away.

## ~ Three ~
### The end of Rangoon

The shooting on Christmas day had more than one outcome. Initially, husband and wife had a furious row in the bedroom: Jean shrieked that he didn't have to kill the man, and he told her she didn't understand the dangers of a city at war. She knew he'd never back down and couldn't bring herself to lie beside him that night, so took herself off to sleep on the lounge sofa.

Deepa found her there the following morning. 'Sorry, madam,' she said.

The maid didn't say what she was sorry about and Jean didn't ask. She'd started to feel that Deepa knew instinctively what her memsahib was feeling.

Jean moved back into their shared bedroom the following night, thinking that too much was happening to complicate their lives further. For the time being she and Philip needed each other, in practical ways at least. But there were longer-term implications and for the first time in three and a half years of marriage she began to turn them over in her head.

The morning after the shooting she went into the bathroom and looked at herself in the mirror. This was unusual. She knew other women gazed at their own reflections. Some did little else. They admired them or found fault with them, pampered their skin, tried out different make-up and hair-styles. But Jean had never been vain about her appearance. She didn't wear make-up and her hair was much as it had been at 14.

What she saw in the bathroom mirror was a slim, 24-year old woman, just over five feet five inches tall. The non-styled hair was short and fell around the sides of her face. She had clean-cut features and very clear brown eyes – a sort of outdoor face. Maybe something more sensual could be made of it if she put in the time and effort, but that had never been a preoccupation. It still wasn't, but she stayed before the mirror as though studying her reflection could help her identify character flaws.

Why had she married Philip? Was she so empty-headed that the decision had been a mere product of time and place? She came from a military family, her father having carried the rank of general. Raised in India under strict conditions of racial segregation, she'd had a limited choice of officer suitors (other ranks clearly out of the question). She'd not questioned the assumption that she would marry in her early 20s, because all her friends did. The life-style of military wives was what she knew and it didn't seem an unpleasant proposition. Philip had been a promising young lieutenant and it was natural for them to come together. He liked her energy – long-distance cycling was her passion –

and she found his lean figure perfectly acceptable; at least, he didn't repel her, as some other young officers did. She was aware of his peremptory manner, of course, but ascribed it to the military life-style. And it was softened by a sense of humour, all the more acceptable coming from such a surprising source.

Like most of her set she'd known little about sex. Conversations with the other girls had been about whether men were good-looking or nice or had prospects. She'd assumed it would be all right when she and Philip got between the sheets. In the event she found the routines of intimacy rather boring, but they didn't take up much time and he seemed satisfied enough.

Until December 23, life as a soldier's wife in Burma had been uneventful. With a houseful of servants she didn't actually *have* to do anything for herself. She didn't even sew or knit like other expatriate women. But she read a great deal and went for long walks around Rangoon (the latter activity now curtailed). She wrote letters to her parents in India. She listened to the gossip of wives in the Pegu Club but rarely contributed to it. The three half-days of work at the hospital afforded a contrast to all this self-indulgence, but even they were fairly predictable once she'd settled in.

The first air raid changed all that. In a single hour Rangoon was transformed from a safe environment to an ugly, violent one in which both present and future were unpredictable. The most disturbing aspect of this, which Jean would hardly admit to herself, was that she'd begun to relish the new uncertainty. At last the daily options were not set out in all their tiresome uniformity. Anything could happen and frequently did. Like a creature emerging from hibernation she felt her imagination stirring, her intellect – long dormant – figuring the possibilities. She relished the chance to be part of it all. She deflected her father's increasingly urgent demands that she return 'home' to India and told Philip she'd stay as long as possible.

In the third week of February, Matron got on her case. 'Tell me your plans, nurse Costain,' she said one afternoon, brusque as ever. 'I assume you have some.'

'What do you mean, Matron?'

'Things won't stay like this for ever – you must realise that. What are the other military wives doing?'

'Oh, them. A lot have left. They take the boats to Calcutta.'

'Then I'll ask again. What are *your* plans?'

'I'm not sure. I'd like to go on working here if I can be useful.'

'You know very well you're useful here, you stupid girl. I don't mean that. A young woman like you won't want to be in Rangoon if the Japanese march in.'

Jean didn't react to the 'stupid girl' comment; she was getting used to Matron's little ways. 'My husband's an intelligence officer. He'll know when it's time.'

'You think so? One thing about war is that nobody knows anything.'

'No, Matron.'

The woman glared at her. 'All right, carry on then.'

At home that evening Jean did sit down and think about her situation, which she supposed was what Matron had intended; the woman might be a fierce old bag but she'd knocked around the world and could be quite astute. As it happened there were good reasons to stick around, apart from not wanting to 'run home to daddy'. Against all the odds

Deepa's husband was still clinging to life in his hospital bed, and Jean had no intention of abandoning her maid at such a time. In the preceding six weeks the two women had grown closer. As relations with Philip cooled, Deepa's calmness and innate good sense meant a lot to her. She'd have described Deepa as a friend, had that not run counter to her entire life experience. She quailed to think of reactions at the Pegu Club had she put that particular thought into words. It would have been more acceptable socially for Jean to take an interest in Jyoti, but so far her efforts in that direction hadn't been reciprocated. She'd tried to engage the girl in conversation but Jyoti remained a distant figure: polite, articulate, and securely locked away with her own thoughts.

Another reason for Jean to stay on was that Indians who'd left Rangoon were steadily coming back, restoring some air of normality to the place. The big exodus had followed the bombings on 23 and 25 December. Understandably, that slowed when no further air-raids materialised. Less clear to her was *why* the refugees were returning. She asked Philip about it one morning at breakfast.

'Because we got into the act,' he told her.

'We?'

'The military, of course. Civic responsibilities were left with the Governor for far too long. The man doesn't know his backside from his elbow.' For once Philip seemed happy to impart information, seizing almost with relief upon something impersonal to talk about. 'Nothing works in Rangoon without the Indians, you must know that. They made up more than half the population. They handled all the nasty, dirty jobs the Burmans were too idle to take on, the docks above all. Shipping has ground to a halt without Indian labour.'

'I can see why the government wanted them,' Jean said, 'But not why they'd want to return.'

'Who knows what goes on in an Indian mind?'

'*Philip*.' She nodded in the direction of Deepa, who was just about within earshot.

He put on his 'exasperated' look. 'Have you heard of Robert Hutchings?'

'No.'

'Why aren't I surprised? He's the Government of India agent here. We got after him, not before time. Hutchings and his men have been patrolling the Prome Road, persuading Indians to come back.'

'All right, but then why did they?'

He laughed, not very nicely. 'I don't think they found it was much fun being evacuees. But apart from that, they're being offered security in government camps. We set them up in the north of the city. And a promise of official evacuation, if it's ever needed.'

'I see.' She thought for a moment. 'Tell me, Philip, what would *you* do if you were an Indian who'd left Rangoon?'

'I don't think like an Indian, I'm profoundly grateful to say.'

'For god's sake!' Red spots of anger sprang up on both her cheeks. She'd begun to hate his utter disregard for those who weren't his own kind.

'All right,' he said slowly, 'Keep your hair on. If I were an Indian who'd left? I'd keep going.'

'But why?'

For one thing, the people who leave early have the best chance of getting through. Trains and steamers are still operating. The roads are fairly clear. The villages still have food to sell. The longer it goes on – with the monsoon on the way, don't forget – the harder it'll get. And anyway – do not repeat this, Jean – I wouldn't want to believe a word this government says. Besides...when there's a war on, nobody knows anything very much.'

'No, Matron.'

'*What!*'

She grinned. 'It was just something Matron said the other day.'

Rangoon functioned more or less normally until mid-February. Admittedly its wealthier citizens began to look decidedly scruffy, as the entire *dhobi* class had disappeared and clothes didn't get ironed. But the population still had drinking water and the phones had come back. The English-language newspapers continued to publish, so foreign residents had some idea what was going on.

The change, when it came, was precipitous. The real blow occurred when the banks closed down and moved up to Mandalay, signalling the beginning of the end. Then the *Rangoon Times* and *New light of Burma* ceased publication and – as always happens in such circumstances – rumours began to flourish. Many of them concerned the British forces facing the Japanese across the river Sittaing, to the north-east of Rangoon. There was never enough detail for a convincing picture, but the situation was clearly unpromising. And one thing everyone knew was that defeat on the Sittaing would bring the Japanese marching into Rangoon.

On the evening of 19 February Philip arrived home late with some hard news: the following day notices were to go up on all public buildings, giving the entire population two days to evacuate.

'This is it, Jean,' he told her. 'You mustn't delay any longer. I *have* to stick around here – our lot will be the last out – but you can't. You can't.'

'You know why I've stayed on,' she said.

'I do know. Look, it's a difficult situation for you.' He was quieter than usual, and more sympathetic. 'You've done all you can – more than most people would. In the end Deepa must make her own decision.'

Still she was undecided. They talked about ways she might leave. Flying from Rangoon was an impossible option with the Japanese in control of the air. Philip thought he could get her out to Calcutta, but the boats taking refugees were getting ridiculously over-crowded.

'What about my jeep?' she said.

'The jeep! You can't get out of Burma in that thing.'

'No, but until I leave – can I use it?'

He sighed. 'Any vehicles left in Rangoon from now on must have a big letter 'E' on their windscreen, or the owners'll be in trouble.' He sighed again. 'All right, I can fix that for you. For a few days. After that...well, you won't be here Jean, will you?'

'No, of course I won't.'

But a week later she *was* still there. She and a mere handful of others, she reflected, driving to and from the hospital through Rangoon's ghostly streets with only the dogs and the undesirables for company. By now Jean was praying that Deepa's husband would die. The thought brought guilt in its wake but the point was, she knew he was going to. Matron had confirmed it and she thought even Deepa knew the truth. In which case why didn't the poor man *get a move on*. They all needed him dead.

By this time she and Philip did little except work. Their social life had dried up on Christmas night, in the slit trenches of the Minto Mansions hotel. Philip was utterly consumed by his job with the 'last-ditchers' (as his outfit had become known), keeping the city's basic services running. Jean worked long hours at the hospital helping Matron tackle emergencies with a diminishing band of nurses.

On 23 February rumours began to filter through of a disaster on the river Sittaing. It seemed the British had blown the bridge with most of their own forces on the wrong (ie east) side. Chaos had ensued. Hundreds died trying to swim the river under fire from Japanese rifles. Now everyone expected the enemy to be in the capital within a fortnight.

On 27 February, Deepa's husband died. Jean came on duty at the hospital and found his bed empty, the body already despatched to the mortuary. Deepa received the news stoically. Her grieving had been done during the long weeks when hope ebbed away. Jean saw no tears from little Jyoti either.

Then came the brou-ha-ha of the Hindu funeral. The Indian funeral grounds were still operating in theory, but there was a 2-day delay while they located a missing employee, the untouchable who tended the funeral pyre. Jean found it strange that this mattered so much when other rituals had been thrown to the winds. They had no male mourners, for a start, so the women of the family attended the burning. And strangest of all she herself – a white, allegedly Christian woman – was allowed to join them.

Only the three of them were present: herself and Deepa – and Jyoti, since Hindus believed in familiarising children with the idea of death. They stood by the pyre on a sunny morning, listened to the crackling of burning wood and felt the heat as Subhas's body was consumed. Deepa enacted the role that normally fell to the eldest son, grasping a long bamboo stick and with one blow cracking her husband's skull, made brittle by the flames. There was something timeless about her upright, unflinching figure as it conducted this ancient ceremony. Jean had never admired her stalwart maid more. Jyoti stood close beside her mother as if her slender arms could offer support. She gave no sign as the skull shattered.

'Are you all right, Jyoti?' Jean asked as they walked to the jeep afterwards.

'Yes, madam.'

'I'm sorry. I'm sorry about your father.'

'His soul has flown free from his body,' the girl said.

'Of course.'

The Hindu funeral rituals seemed quaint but Jean assumed they served a purpose. She was used to hospital death, the unsentimental kind. Of course she had no conception of what lay ahead: mortality in all its infinite variety, unattended, unmourned.

The next morning when Philip had left for work she and Deepa sat down at the kitchen table; this happened naturally now, without urging on her part.

'Are you all right, Deepa? Jean began.

'All right, madam.'

'Are you sure?'

'Yes, sure.' The maid gave a little nod. 'Over now.'

'Yes, it's over. Awful for you. And Jyoti?'

'All right also. I told her it will happen.'

'I see.' Jean sought the right words. 'I never know. She seems so...I don't know, so serious...I never know what she's thinking.'

'Sometimes *I* don't know. Not easy for Indian girl in Burma.' Deepa clasped her arms across her breasts. 'She keeps everything here inside – like me.'

At this Deepa turned and bestowed upon her employer an unstudied smile so radiant that for a moment Jean imagined her body had been warmed by it. She thought that the moment Subhas first saw this smile he would have been utterly lost. She also reflected that she and Deepa had managed a whole conversation with – if memory served – only one 'madam' in it; and that for the first time ever Deepa had revealed something about herself; and that she'd spoken in a normal voice, not as servant to employer.

'I wish I could do more for her,' said Jean, Jyoti still on her mind. 'I'd like to help, wherever I can.'

'You *do* help,' Deepa said.

'I don't know. I never feel I've established contact with her.'

'It's good, madam, really. She likes you.'

'D'you think so?'

'Of course. I know her.'

Jean looked around, taking in the familiar surroundings of the kitchen, her domain and Deepa's: the dinner set she'd taken there from India, the rack of sharp knives, the new-fangled tin-opener fixed to the wall; all soon to be left behind.

'Deepa, there's something we need to talk about.' She dreaded this conversation because it involved a decision on her own part that she wasn't ready to make. 'If I leave Rangoon...'

'You *must* leave.'

'OK then, when I leave...what will you do?  What are your plans...now that you don't have Subhas?  Can you stay on in your old house?'

Deepa shook her head almost violently.  'Rangoon not good place for Indians now.  All leaving.'

'Because of the Japanese coming?'

The maid shrugged.  'Japanese maybe...we don't know.  The Burmans they kill many Indians.  No good without the British.'

This was as Philip had predicted.  'But *how* would you go?' Jean asked.

Deepa shrugged again and turned towards the kitchen window.  On the road to Prome the Indian exodus had resumed more extravagantly than ever.  The sound of it was a constant accompaniment to their lives: the tramp of feet, creaking of wooden carts, wailing of women or babies.

'Walk, madam,' Deepa said.

'Walk!  On your own!  Are there friends you could go with?  *Where* would you go?'

Deepa shook her head.  'My friends they leave long time.  I go with Jyoti.  It's all right, madam, all Indians doing this.  I have sister living in Assam.  We go there.  My mother and father they are dead.'

'Oh Deepa,' was all Jean could say.  She could not envisage Deepa and Jyoti setting off on the mammoth journey to India.  'We'll talk again,' she ended lamely.

Until Philip returned that evening Jean's thoughts were in turmoil.

For once she'd taken a day off, at Matron's insistence, and now wished she were back at the hospital with other matters to absorb her. An idea was forming in her head: one that would turn life upside down and expose her to hazards she could only guess at; that would leave wives at the club open-mouthed and send Philip into a rage. 'It's not my fault,' she said out loud, rehearsing an argument with him. 'I didn't choose this place or these times. I'm doing what I can.' And she thought 'Am I crazy or what? I'm a feather-brained young girl who's never questioned the world I came out of; who doesn't begin to understand other races even when she lives in their country.'

Philip came in at ten. He looked exhausted in a dirty, sweat-stained uniform. Before she could speak he launched into a diatribe about his day. He'd been at the rail station controlling the exit of refugees.

'It's pandemonium out there,' he said. 'Too many people, too few trains. We've had one hell of a job keeping order. No-one's allowed more than one piece of luggage yet you've got people trying to put half their household on board. One bloke went berserk – shoving women and kids, trampling people under foot. I had to let fly with my lathi – knocked him out cold.'

'I've been talking to Deepa,' Jean broke in without ceremony. 'About her plans now that...you know, now that her husband's dead. She's thinking of walking out of Rangoon with her daughter.'

'Of course she is. They are all. What else could she do?'

'The thing is...' Even then Jean wasn't sure what she was going to say. That's what drives men crazy, she thought; that women don't know what they're going to do until the moment they do it. 'The thing is...I'm thinking of going with them.'

She knew it was hopelessly ill-managed: she hadn't prepared the way; he was tired and irritable; she'd not even got a beer down him. He sniggered, then laughed out loud; looked at her and laughed again. 'Don't be so bloody ridiculous.'

His reaction spurred her on. 'I'm serious.'

In their four years of marriage Philip had never laid a hand on her. She knew of at least two officers who mistreated their wives, but Philip had always controlled his temper. Until now. He took hold of her shoulders and shook her violently back and forth till she felt her teeth were rattling.

'*Do-not-be-a-stupid-little-girl*. I'm at my wits' end with all I have to do. I don't need you playing games on top of it.'

'I'm reducing your burden,' she said, more calmly than she felt. 'I'll be making my own way out.'

'*Three women! Hah!*'

'Thank you for your vote of confidence, Philip. Half of those leaving the city are women.'

'Yes and most of them will die. Be sensible. You can't possibly walk all that way.'

'I don't intend to. I'm taking the jeep as far as Prome. We should be able to pick up a paddle-steamer there.'

'You'd be at the back of a very long queue. There'd be some surprises in store for you, my girl.' He swung round with a dismissive gesture. 'Why am I even talking about this...this ludicrous pipe dream?'

'I know there'll be a log-jam of people for the boats,' she said equably. 'That's where I come in. Deepa on her own – of course it would be difficult. But travelling with an English memsahib. I owe it to her, Philip.

I can't just abandon her. It's not as if you could get the three of us on a boat to Calcutta.'

'I'd have a job getting *you* a berth, you've left it so long. And they're not giving Indians deck places any more.'

'There you are then. Anyway, according to the wireless the Japanese are taking women off ships going to Calcutta. Is that true?'

He was silent.

'Exactly. I don't fancy that, thank you very much. No, we're going north. You keep telling me to leave. Now I am.'

'Sit down.' He thrust her into a kitchen chair, a more violent version of what she'd once done with Deepa. 'It's time you heard some home truths.' He could barely stand from exhaustion but his eyes still blazed with intelligence. She felt for him; wives were supposed to do what their husbands said. He was shouting in a way she'd never heard, stressing every other word in a sort of rhythmic chant. 'It's a thousand miles to the Indian border. A thousand miles of country you don't know. All you know is a nice little rail trip to Mandalay. There'd be hordes of refugees contesting every step of the way with you. You'd run out of food. Above all you'd run out of water. There'll be Japs everywhere and if they don't get you the dacoits will, because at times like this every Burman becomes a dacoit. Further north – if you made it that far, which I doubt – is the jungle. You have *no idea* what that's like – some of the worst terrain in the world. The heat alone is a killer. The area's infested with malaria. The leeches will drive you insane. No roads, just paths.' He paused for a moment before completing the rant in a voice that rose to a crescendo. 'And there's the monsoon, Jean – you haven't even thought about that. Believe me, once that comes down the whole place is impassable. Don't even think about it. You'll be lost and hungry and ill and utterly exhausted. You'll just want to *lay down and die*.'

'Then I'd better get moving, hadn't I?' she said.

There was no more conversation that night. Philip bathed and ate, then they lay on opposite sides of the bed with the unspoken thoughts between them. Jean woke at 5am. She stayed where she was with Philip's tirade running through her head and the thin dawn light filtering through the window. If there was a time when she wavered it was then. She'd said nothing to Deepa; she could still bid her maid goodbye and join the few remaining expats scrambling to escape – by which route she knew not.

But the truth was she *wanted* to leave with Deepa. She was in a peculiar, fatalistic mood. Of course she shrank from the dangers Philip had enumerated, but irrationally she also relished the challenge. She wanted to prevail against the impossible. She'd had things too easy, like most of her kind. Well this was different. It could be the end of her – she was clear-eyed about that. But she had no children and only half a marriage, not much to lose. There were her parents, of course, but returning to India would be just a reprise of failure and disenchantment.

By the time she rose at 7am her head was clear. She went to the kitchen where Deepa was already at work and described what she intended to do. The maid was astounded and sat down abruptly in the manner of someone who'd received bad news. Then she rallied and began to argue, urging her employer to other courses of action.

Eventually Jean took Deepa's hands in both of hers. 'Look, I don't want to do this if it's against your wishes,' she said. 'Now tell me honestly if you and Jyoti would prefer to do this on your own. Tell me what you really think.'

Deepa hesitated for a moment. 'No madam.'

'No, what? What do you mean?'

'We don't want to go alone.'

'Well then...that's it. We're agreed.'

'If madam thinks...' Now Deepa smiled her irresistible smile. 'Yes. Yes, we will try, together.'

Later Philip sprang a surprise by calling in mid-morning, something Jean couldn't remember happening before. They confronted each other awkwardly on the front porch.

'Are you still determined to go?' he asked quietly.

'Yes Philip. I'm sorry.'

'When will you leave?'

'A couple of days, probably. I need to call at the hospital, clear things with Matron.'

'Don't leave it too long. A few more days and the Japs will be on the door-step. Just a minute, I've got something for you.'

He went to his jeep and returned with three water-bags. 'You'll need something like this out there. Whatever else you jettison, hang on to these. They're a bit big for thingy...the girl...'

'Jyoti.'

'Yes, Jyoti – but she doesn't have to fill it to the brim.'

Her eyes filled up, that he was still looking out for her. 'Philip, that is so very kind of you.'

'There's something else.' He was brisk but conciliatory, as if anxious to atone for the previous evening. 'Come round the back for a minute.'

He led her to the no-man's land at the back of the bungalow. Her curiosity was pricked as he took four empty beer bottles from a cardboard box and placed them at intervals on the low wall marking the end of their territory.

'Got pie-eyed preparing these,' he said.

She grinned. 'What *are* you doing?'

'It's a dangerous world where you're going. I want you to take this.' She stepped back a pace back as he drew a .45 revolver from his pocket. 'I believe it's technically a court-martial offence to give this to someone else, but to hell with it. The rule book's out of the window. Now, let's move back a bit – say 20 yards.' He took her arm and they retreated a distance from the wall. 'OK, now take a close look at the way I'm standing.'

He moved the safety switch, aimed and pressed the trigger. Birds rose from the trees all around and Deepa emerged from the bungalow to watch. His first shot missed, but the second smashed the bottle to smithereens.

'Now you have a go.' He put the gun carefully into her hand. 'When you're not actually going to fire, always point it away from you – towards the ground, preferably. Now try to stay relaxed, and hold your breath as you squeeze the trigger.'

Jean raised the gun and fired. A bottle leapt into the air and disintegrated.

'Well done, you,' he said. 'I reckon you could pick this up quite quickly.'

She fired twice more and the two remaining bottles smashed to pieces.

He looked at her accusingly. 'You little devil. You can shoot already.'

She laughed. 'I'm sorry, Philip. I couldn't resist it. My father taught me. He always said aim slightly above the target, as the bullet drops.'

'Just so. I should've guessed. Anyway I feel a whole lot better now I know you can handle a fire-arm.' He handed over a small box of ammunition. 'Should be enough there for any eventuality.'

Impulsively she took a step forward and kissed his cheek. 'Thank you so much.'

'Before I get back to work, could we talk about your route?' His whole attitude to her had changed, she noted; he was almost deferential. 'To tell the truth I've no idea what to advise, the picture's changing so quickly – but there is one thing. A lot of the early leavers are going via the Arakan hills. You'll probably see them crossing the Irrawaddy at Prome. They aim to go through the Arakan to Taungup, then get a country boat to Akyab. From there, big coastal ships to Chittagong.'

Jean was loath to comment and reveal her ignorance, but she did know where Akyab was.

'Quite a short route then,' she said brightly.

He nodded. 'It's tempting for that reason. But the thing is, a lot of Indians are dying on that route. Nobody knows how many, of course, but we hear stories from those who've turned back. It's not a good scene. You need to know that.'

'Thank you Philip. I won't go there, I promise.'

He nodded. 'Please don't. Whichever route you take, you'll have to find your own way to Prome first.'

'Yes, I'm taking the jeep. That is...unless I can get a paddle-steamer from here.'

He shook his head. 'They've all been sent up-river. We'd have preferred to take them out to sea, in spite of the risks, but they'll be needed. Churchill's sent an order – hold on to Burma at all costs.'

'It's the jeep, then.'

'After Prome, you'll have to play it by ear. Depends on where the Japs are, where our forces are, what transport is still operational. There's an airport at Myitkyina in the north – it's still working at present. Train goes there from near Mandalay. That's one possibility. Or via the river Chindwin to Kalewa, then walk out to Assam. But who knows. Keep your ear to the ground, Jean. Ask the people you meet. No-one's going to have definite information but you'll build up a picture.' He touched her arm with an affectionate gesture. 'OK, see you later.'

Jean drove to the hospital, thinking about it being the last day she'd work there. She was sorry to be leaving Matron in the lurch, but the work-load had calmed down in recent weeks. She assumed they'd seen the last of the air raids as there'd been none since Christmas day.

She found Matron in the office and described her intention to leave.

'It's about time,' the woman said. 'Right then, if we're to have the pleasure of your company today, you'd better get cracking. Go to ward 4.'

'There is one thing, Matron.' Jean hesitated, though she'd already planned to make her request. 'I wonder if...is there any chance you could let me have some Mecrapine for the journey? I think we'll be walking through some bad country.'

The woman glared, making her eyes look more Chinese than ever. 'Do you regard this hospital as a pharmaceutical store, nurse Costain?'

'No, of course not, Matron.'

'I should think not indeed. Go on, get to work. And make sure you say goodbye before you leave.'

'Yes Matron.'

Jean spent the day in the now-familiar tasks, saying her farewells to the few remaining people she knew. Unexpectedly, she felt rather sad to be leaving. 'Ridiculous,' she told herself, 'Moping over this place of pain and death.' She worked her usual shift and then some, determined not to give Matron – 'that old bat' was her thought – any cause for complaint. Well after seven she reported to the office.

'Well, that's it,' Matron said. 'Thank you for the work you've done here, Nurse Costain. Most of it has been well up to standard.'

'Thank you, Matron.'

'Now then.' The woman took a package from her desk and handed it over. Jean heard the thing clink. 'This is some of what the hospital owes you. It's quite heavy, but you'll find coins more use than paper money where you're going.'

'But how...' Jean blurted out. 'I mean, the banks are closed, aren't they?'

'There are ways and means. There's also a piece of paper here promising the residue of what we owe. You'll find it utterly useless.'

'Thank you, Matron. Thank you very much.'

Another package came out of the desk drawer. 'Here is some Mecrapine,' the older woman said. 'Make sure all three of your party take a tablet every day. Malaria can be lethal. There are a few other bits and pieces, including some chlorine for the water. Be very careful about boiling everything you drink. There are rumours of cholera in the Prome area.'

Jean wanted to speak but the words wouldn't come.  Tears were running down both sides of her face.  She tried mopping them up, to no avail.

'Now don't be silly, Nurse Costain.'

She never did manage a 'thank-you' for the tablets, but she snivelled 'What about you, Matron?  What will you do?'

'I shall stay here, of course.'

'But...will you be safe?'

'Certainly.  The Japanese aren't going to bother with an old bat like me.'

Through her tears Jean couldn't repress a smile.

'What is it, nurse?  Do you recognise that description of me?'

'Of course not, Matron, I...oh!'  More tears defeated her attempt to continue.

Matron held out a hand.  'Good luck.  It's Jean, isn't it?'

'Yes!'

'I'm Peggy.'

**~ Four ~**

**On the road to Prome**


Two days later Jean left Rangoon with Deepa and Jyoti, in a jeep piled high with too many possessions. She'd found packing for the journey an intractable task. There was no telling how long the vehicle would last, and once it was abandoned they'd be limited to what could be carried. Even so, she found herself reluctant to leave certain things behind. Of the two of them, Deepa had been far more practical. She'd insisted on ground sheets, mosquito nets, changes of clothes, and above all sturdy footwear. And blankets, because the nights were cold whatever the daytime temperatures. They had a metal mug and plate each and a small stove. There were plenty of tinned goods that would be of no use once they left the jeep, but apart from that rice – inevitably – was the main food component. Jean had no idea whether petrol would be available en route and Philip came up with two large cans of it to go in the boot. At the last minute she remembered to take along Philip's revolver.

Saying goodbye to him was a sad, muted business. They'd rarely been separated for long in the previous four years and the moment of parting was more difficult than she'd anticipated. But she had to leave and he had to stay.

He helped her to load the car then stood by awkwardly. 'I suppose this is it,' he said. 'I wish I could come with you.'

'Me too. But you have your job to do.' She put a hand on his arm and stood up close. Their bitter disagreements were running through her mind. 'I'm sorry Philip.'

'Don't.' He pasted on an unconvincing smile. 'We'll get back to how we were. And you'll be all right, a resourceful woman like you.'

Of course he knew better than most the risks she faced. In the past he'd always been the one facing danger. Now it was both of them.

'What about you?' she said. 'What will happen now?'

'Our job's almost done. They reckon the Japs will be here in a few days. The plan is to take us last-ditchers off from the docks. Those boats are getting very crowded though, so we'll have to see.'

She pressed forward and kissed him on the mouth. 'I can't stand this,' she said, 'Let's not prolong it. We'll meet again soon.'

She climbed into the jeep and started the ignition. He stood aside without acknowledging Deepa and Jyoti. As the vehicle moved off she saw his figure in the rear-view mirror, amongst scattered groups of Indians tramping towards Prome.

Jean had thought of getting to Prome in a day, but soon had to revise the plan. The Prome Road, in poor condition at the best of times, was hopelessly congested with the Indian exodus. Carts and pedestrians alike spilled across the highway forcing the jeep onto the verge. Every so often she was obliged to stop whilst a knot of refugees cleared in response to her hooter. They passed some dismal sights. Several of the older people were flagging already and it seemed inconceivable they could reach Prome, let alone India. Children looked perkier but surely lacked the stamina that would be needed. One striking image – a barefoot old man with a bamboo pole slung across his shoulders, at each end of it a pannier containing a small infant – symbolised the hopeless courage of the communal endeavour.

Some of the wooden carts on the road did not inspire confidence. One of them ran on two gigantic wheels as tall as the men who were pulling it; a contraption piled high with sacks of provisions, these surmounted by half-a-dozen women, one holding aloft an open umbrella. Overloading was a common failing, Jean thought, reflecting on her own efforts. People had been as loath as she was to part with prized possessions, some of them quite ludicrous. She spotted a child's doll-house on one cart, a framed picture of Krishna on another. One family had taken along a typewriter.

They were travelling with the jeep's canvas roof down, and Jean wondered how Deepa felt as she sailed in full view past her toiling compatriots. She hoped the maid would not recognise any acquaintances, because she'd no intention of taking more people on board. It was clear to her already that an element of selfishness was needed if they were to get out of Burma. And here she was doing the easiest part of it: a spin in the jeep along a reasonable road, in mild sunshine.

After four hours Jean pulled them 20 yards off the tarmac onto a patch of ground bordering the paddy fields. They ate food prepared earlier: sandwiches for Jean, samosas for Deepa and Jyoti. Again Jean thought 'It's never going to be any simpler than it is now'. The flat fields stretched away on all sides, with the stubbly remains of rice crop poking above the soil. Nearby, the conveyor belt of refugees toiled past with their staves and bundles and bunches of dry wood.

Jyoti had travelled in silent isolation at the back of the jeep, upright and composed. Not for the first time Jean wished she could hit it off with the girl – something, at least, beyond their usual polite exchange of formalities.

'Is everything all right, Jyoti?' she said.

'Yes, madam.'

'Is there anything you need?'

'No thank you. Except...'

She spoke some Hindi with her mother, then climbed down and squatted without fuss to pee, using the vehicle as cover. As she did so a droning sound signalled the first Japanese plane Jean had seen in two months. It coasted above them, dipping down along the road so the pilot could reconnoitre. Immediately a chorus of wailing emanated from the refugee column and rose to an unnerving crescendo, subsiding only as the aircraft became a distant speck on the horizon. Jean remembered what Philip had told her about Japanese mastery of the skies. The incident gave her a sense of their vulnerability to air attack in such a flat landscape.

Around 5pm she felt she couldn't safely drive any further. Nine hours at the wheel was quite a stint for a woman accustomed to short journeys around Rangoon. Dusk was near and the engine had developed an odd little blip, suggesting that the jeep also needed a rest. The milometer told her they were about half-way to Prome.

'I'm thinking of stopping round here,' she told Deepa.

Deepa nodded. 'This is a good place. We can get off the road.' She indicated a patch of wispy trees set in scrub-land on one side of the highway. 'Hide behind the trees.'

'Do you think we need to hide?' Jean asked.

Deepa hesitated, as she always did before reporting violence against the Indian community. 'It's better. Many Burmans attack Indians on this road. Kill the people, take everything.'

'Good lord, Deepa! We can have the hood up.'

'Hood soft, madam. They cut with *dahs*.' She imitated someone cutting through a canvas roof.

'You've got me worried now. Do you think we ought to keep watch then?'

'Better, yes. You, me – half night each. This place very dangerous.'

Jean manoeuvred the jeep round the back of the trees. Sure enough they provided effective cover against anyone approaching from the road. Once darkness came down the camouflage was complete, though they could see the pinpricks of light from dozens of stoves as refugees prepared their evening meals. The aroma of food drifting through the trees sparked their own appetites. Jean took the paraffin stove from the boot and she and Deepa prepared some rice and tinned sausages for three. It was the first time the two women had cooked together and it came naturally. Deepa had a knack of combining quickly and gracefully with other people. Jyoti contributed – unasked – by making a sort of table from stuff in the jeep, so they could sit and eat from it. They lit a couple of coils to keep mosquitoes at bay.

In the circumstances the three of them communicated pretty well. Jean had made a big effort to learn Burmese during her three and a half years in the country and could usually make herself understood. She asked the others to use their Burmese for at least some of the time, and they obliged. Jyoti was the star linguist, speaking both Burmese and English (and of course Hindi) in the clear, confident tone of a child. Jean made them laugh by rolling her head in Indian fashion and throwing a Hindi '*acha*' into the conversation; she knew it as one of those meaningless expressions like 'now then' in English, or '*ya'ani*' in Arabic.

Moving from the formal atmosphere of the bungalow (with Patrick hovering in the background) to a small wood off the Prome Road had demolished some of the barriers between them. It was more like a jolly picnic than a nocturnal meal on a desperate flight from Japanese invaders. The two Indians made fun of Jean's cross-legged posture, and when Jean dropped a piece of sausage into her mug of water it convulsed all three of them. For the first time she heard Jyoti laugh – a sweet, trilling sound that transformed the girl's serious little face. She thought: 'I'm glad I came. Whatever happens now...*whatever* happens...I've made the right decision.'

They retired for the night after eating. Deepa repeated her view that someone should keep watch, and Jean volunteered to take the first shift. She sat on the running board of the jeep shrouded in a blanket and mosquito net while Deepa and Jyoti stretched out on the seats inside.

She was soon glad of the blanket. This surprised her a little, given the warmth of the day, but the night chill slowly insinuated itself into her bones. After an hour she opened the boot – quietly, to avoid waking the others – and removed some warmer clothing (plus something soft to sit on, as the running board was chafing her bony rump). She settled again and sat there with her thoughts. In the moonlight the ranks of thin trees were a ghostly presence. Large bats flitted incessantly above. She might have enjoyed the sense of solitude but for the overwhelming din of the cicadas.

It would have been difficult to sleep properly on the running board but she did find herself nodding off, then jerking into consciousness. On one of these occasions she snapped awake with a distinct sense of having missed something. She stared wildly around but noticed nothing unusual. Her wrist-watch showed 1am – an hour before Deepa would take over for the second shift. She stood up stiffly and walked a few paces towards the trees, listening acutely. Then it came – the thing she'd missed before – the unmistakable sound of someone approaching through the wood. Jean strained her eyes, imagining all sorts of things. The movements came steadily closer. Her heart was beating like mad. She felt the weight of the revolver in her pocket and drew it out, adjusting the safety catch and raising her right hand to aim into the amorphous darkness.

As she stood trembling with apprehension Jean felt a small, warm hand slide into her own. Jyoti had emerged from the jeep – soundlessly, in the manner of her mother – and moved to where Jean stood. Jean gave the hand a squeeze and bent to hear the girl's whispered question.

'Are you frightened, Jean?'

'Yes, I am. Are you?'

'Not when I'm with you,' the girl said. Then, 'Have you shot anyone before?'

'No, and I don't want to start now.'

'But if we have to?'

'Let's hope we don't,' Jean whispered, going down onto her haunches so she could put her arm round the girl and her cheek against Jyoti's cheek. Her heart was singing; there was no other word for it.

The sounds were closer now. There could be no doubt someone was approaching the jeep, yet still they saw nothing. The wood presented a thousand shades and illusions.

Two things happened at once. An abrupt, truly shocking sound – the braying of a mule – rent the air, silencing (or so it seemed) even the cicadas. And a mule's head loomed from the trees a few feet in front of them. Then another sound – the trilling of Jyoti's laughter, which came again and again until tears ran down the girl's face and Jean's own laugh joined in.

'That is a very lucky mule,' Jean said. 'I was in such a blue funk I could easily have shot him.'

'What is a blue funk, Jean?'

Jean grinned and kissed Jyoti's cheek. 'It means I was very scared. My goodness, I'm going to teach you such a lot of English, just you watch out.'

'I want to learn it.'

Then Deepa came out of the jeep, woken (as who wouldn't be) by the mule's braying, and took over the watch. Jean lay herself down in the front seat and the sleep she craved came quickly. Just before dropping off she heard Jyoti's small voice from the back.

'Very funny.'

The next morning they got going early, after a drink of tea. It was all but impossible to be on the road before other Indians but the route did seem less congested, perhaps because they were further away from Rangoon. Jean had high hopes of reaching Prome before dark. Her main concern was the jeep, which again gave occasional blips as if the petrol supply was being interrupted. There was no point in lifting the hood to look inside; engines were a foreign country where Jean was concerned. For the first time since setting off she thought of Philip, who would have known what to do.

They took an early lunch – again to give the engine a breather – then pressed on. The distance to Prome grew smaller and Jean breathed more easily, but the jeep's hiccuping intensified. She found herself waiting anxiously for each new blip. In mid-afternoon the worst happened. A violent commotion occurred and the engine stalled. A cloud of steam seeped from under the hood. She let the vehicle coast for a few yards until it came to rest at the road-side. They were six miles short of their destination.

'Damn,' she said, a word that seemed entirely inadequate for the situation. 'Damn and blast.'

'Problem, madam?' said Deepa.

Jean spread her hands helplessly. 'I'm so sorry, Deepa. I'm hopeless with machines. I've no idea what to do.'

'I'll ask someone.'

Pedestrian traffic had thinned out considerably, but Indian families still walked past every couple of minutes.  Deepa stood in the road scrutinising each batch of people, then made her move.  The man she approached was heavily laden but walked with a bounce in his step and – even in these circumstances – a grin on his face.  He signalled his wife and child to stop and greeted Jean cheerfully.

'Problem, madam?'

She knew from the way he threw up the hood – which alone would have taken her several minutes – that the Indian knew what he was doing.  He began a systematic check of the engine.  His wife waited submissively and his young daughter talked to Jyoti.  Jean felt embarrassed that this family should be inconvenienced by the English memsahib; the woman who'd coasted past him in a vehicle she was incompetent to handle.  She thought: 'Well, we're all equal now – the whole swarming rabble of us.  Anyone who prospers will do it through gumption and guts, not privilege.'  She'd not known it would come to that, but in a strange way she was glad it had.

The Indian straightened up and shook his head.  'No good, madam, sorry.  Radiator broken.'

'So *that's* it.'

'No water.  Needing new radiator.  No chance here.  Very sorry, madam.'

She thanked the man warmly and used some of their precious water for cleaning his hands.  Offered a choice of items from the jeep he politely declined, saying the family was already overloaded.  He helped her push the vehicle off the road, then went on his way.

Abandoning the jeep was a wrench but Jean was learning to be less sentimental about possessions.  The three of them took as much as could be carried from the vehicle. Jean had a rucksack she'd used in her hill-climbing days, and stuffed the thing with all manner of items. Deepa used a system of carrying things on her head. Water bags were filled from the big container on the vehicle; Jyoti insisted on carrying hers full up.

Jean had always had a passion for physical fitness and was pleased to see that the other two moved easily. The trio's natural pace took them past many of the groups on the road. Jyoti walked as she did everything else, with a self-effacing economy of movement. She and Deepa sometimes resembled two sisters rather than mother and daughter. Of course, Jean reflected, this is a *road*; other surfaces lay in wait for them, a great deal more challenging. All the same she was encouraged by their progress.

They reached the outskirts of Prome just before dark. Immediately the atmosphere of the road – which had been disciplined and quite cheerful – took on a darker tone. At one point where a side road gave easy access to the river, local people had put up a bamboo pole to block the way and were charging Indians one anna each to obtain water. They had no conceivable right to do such a thing but a posse of desperate-looking characters with *dahs* ensured that the refugees paid up. A bit further on a ferry pier reminded Jean of what Philip said – about Indians crossing the river to take the dangerous Arakan route to the coast. Here the baser instincts of human nature were embodied by the police. A gang of them stood across the access point telling refugees that the ferry crossing was forbidden. Closer inspection revealed that eyes were averted if the travellers slipped a bribe into police hands. The rate was said to be one rupee per person. This prompted Deepa to report 'Burmese saying, madam. There is not one dacoit but two – first the dacoit, then the police.'

They camped that night on a little square near the ferry crossing. Despite the jeep disaster, Jean felt optimistic. Breaking down so close to Prome had allowed them to carry many of the things they needed for the last few miles. All three of them were in good spirits. They had money, and the next day she would book them onto a boat up-river.

But when they arrived at the landing-stage the following morning her spirits plunged. A huge concourse – a few thousand at least – was milling around the river bank. Indians were in the majority but she also saw Anglo-Indians, Anglo-Burmans and Gurkhas, and several other nationalities, if foreign languages were any indication. A sprinkling of Burmese police struggled to control the confusion. A great babble of voices permeated the scene. The on-site toilets were hopelessly inadequate and a stench drifted across from a public shitting area somewhere nearby.

Jean threw a helpless look at Deepa. A single paddle-steamer was moored on the river but the prospects of getting on it seemed remote.

'It's all right,' Deepa whispered, leaning forward intimately. 'We are three people.'

'Three amongst three thousand!' Jean exclaimed.

'Odd number,' Deepa insisted. 'Very auspicious.'

Later Jean remembered that the Burmese, an insanely superstitious race, believed odd numbers to be lucky. That would have helped her to appreciate the first joke she'd ever heard from Deepa, at such a time in such a place.

The system for getting onto a boat required passengers to buy tickets from the local agent.   A police presence outside his office ensured that there was that rare Burmese phenomenon, a queue – and a long one at that.  After standing in it for two hours Jean was admitted to see the agent, a Burman.  The minute she laid eyes on the the man she knew a difficult time lay ahead.  He sprawled in his chair scrutinising her with barely disguised malignancy.  She told him she wanted to book three places on a paddle-steamer going up-river.

'And where do you expect to get to?' the man said.

'Well, we'll go as far up-river as we can.'

'As far as you can.'

'That's right.'

He made no reply but sat looking at her.  Jean stared back.  Eventually the Burman raised a hand to indicate the press of people staring through the office windows.  'I suppose you are aware that a very large number of people want places on our boats?'

'One couldn't not be aware.'

'So?'

'So what do I need to do to get tickets?'

The Burman left another silence.  He was enjoying the interview immensely.  'You English,' he said.  'You come here as if you own the country.  Now you have failed to defend us you want a special service to run away.'

'I asked about the system for buying tickets.'

'The system is simple.  I allocate the tickets as necessary.'

'Then what would you advise me to do now?'

'I advise you to queue up again tomorrow.  Who knows – you may even have success.  Now I really must give attention to others – if you will kindly allow me.'

Jean left the office with her cheeks burning. She was thinking: 'Is there no end to my arrogance?'. The Burman had been unpleasant but he had a point. She was used to throwing her weight around, in the nicest possible way of course. Previously, English memsahibs went to the front of any queue. Now the old order was over. She remembered Philip's comment: 'You're in for some surprises, my girl.' Out in the crowd Deepa moved towards her and Jean shook her head. She blushed again, remembering her arrogant assumption that Deepa would profit from a memsahib companion. It was a moot point which racial group was more likely to fuel the Burman's disdain – the English or the Indians.

They camped some distance down the river bank that night to get away from the crush. Even so, few patches of the ground around them remained free of human bodies. The following morning she again queued outside the office, with the same result. Her spirits were plummeting. The country's communications centred on the Irrawaddy, and the impasse over boats left her with few options. There *was* a continuation of the Prome Road running alongside the river, but the three of them couldn't walk the whole way out of Burma. Briefly she wondered whether Mandalay would have been a better objective – till she remembered that the Japanese would be all over that route after the Sittaing débâcle.

On the second day they met up with the Indian who'd been helpful on the Prome Road. Jyoti was getting on well with the young daughter and spent some time with her. The man – who went under the name of Ramesh, Jean discovered – was an enterprising character, the sort who picked up bits of information from all over the place. Like Jean, he'd drawn a blank when dealing with the Burman agent.

'Bad man, madam,' he told her.

'The trouble is,' Jean said, 'There aren't enough boats. He can do as he likes.'

'More boats coming,' Ramesh said, 'But small number. Many were here end of February – people say four hundred. Sent up-river with food supplies.'

Jean shook her head. 'There are too many of us. Too many people. And there's no system for allocating places on boats.'

'Money, madam,' Ramesh said, making the universal finger-rubbing gesture. 'People paying money.'

'You mean bribes?'

'Of course bribes, madam.' Ramesh looked like a man to whom bribes were a familiar coinage. Many people telling me this – they are paying bribes to the Burman.'

The next day, after another lengthy wait outside the agent's office, Jean came straight to the point with the man. 'There are two more boats in today,' she told him. 'Tell me how much I need to pay you to get onto one of them?'

The Burman looked shocked. 'Are you trying to bribe me?'

'What do you think?'

'There are thousands of people waiting out there, and most of them are not wealthy English ladies.'

'Don't be ridiculous. You're growing fat from the bribes people pay. Everyone knows it.' She turned and left the office without giving him the satisfaction of replying.

It was clear to Jean now – three days too late, she thought – that no tickets would be coming her way through the 'proper sources'. In wartime there were no proper sources. She felt increasingly oppressed by their situation, trapped on the bank of the Irrawaddy with no escape outlet. A handful of boats arrived at the landing-stage and departed crammed with refugees, but the numbers who left were exceeded by newcomers piling in off the Prome Road. The river bank was in a horrendous state, defiled by the unavoidable detritus of human existence.

What she felt was akin to claustrophobia: the sense that she would never get away from this place. Absurdly, she was starting to hate the landscape. She'd conceived a dislike for the pagoda that was set back from the east bank on the hillside. She resented the Arakan Yomas as they loomed up behind flat paddy fields. She hated everything about the sprawling, stinky, congested and inescapable scene.

Seeing the Yomas made her think of the ferry. It would be a simple matter to retrace their steps a bit, cross the river and strike out across the mountains to the coast. A lot of Indian refugees were doing just that. But Philip's warning about the Arakan route was still in her head, and there was no point in being married to an intelligence officer if you ignored his advice. There had to be another way.

She took heart from her brief contacts with Ramesh. His situation was worse than hers – he was *Indian*, for god's sake – but he met all reverses with a perky resilience, as if time would resolve them. She started to think seriously about alternative courses of action. If the Burman agent was a dead end, who else had the authority to sanction her passage on a boat? On their fourth day in Prome she contacted the captains of two paddle-steamers berthed on the river. She haggled long and hard without success. Either they were honest men or she didn't have enough cash at her disposal. Later that afternoon she saw an Indian money-lender being ushered aboard one of the boats and decided that ready cash *was* the problem. The next day she tried a third vessel and was again rebuffed.

Her feelings of responsibility for Deepa and Jyoti led her to consider more extreme measures. Desperate measures. An idea was forming, and on their sixth day in Prome she resolved to give it a go. Her worry was, could she actually *do* it; could she deliver? She was in territory that went beyond her wildest and worst dreams. Well, she thought, blanking every negative consideration from her head, there was only one way to find out.

## ~ Five ~
### Paddle-steamer on the Irrawaddy

A new paddle-steamer had docked, and on her seventh morning in Prome Jean went onto the landing-stage to take a look at it. The boat was a large affair with the name 'Flying fish' prominently displayed above the paddles. As yet no passengers had been allowed on board so the only people she could see were crew members. It was the captain she was interested in. After a bit a man emerged from a cabin and stood near the stern smoking a cigarette. She deduced from his manner and the way he treated other crew that this was the person in charge. He'd be a Chittagonian, like most of the steamer captains; a solid-looking figure who ambled about on deck in his own time.

She returned to the patch of river bank where they'd spent the night. Jyoti was playing with her new friend nearby. Deepa sat cross-legged on the grass gazing at the water with the patient demeanour that Jean envied and knew she could never aspire to. The woman even looked ravishing camping out, with none of the usual accoutrements of civilisation on hand.

Jean plonked herself down beside her. 'Deepa, do you have your make-up with you?'

'Make-up?' The Indian looked puzzled and put a hand up to her face. 'You mean...'

'Yes, that make-up.'

'I have of course.'

'Right then, will you do something for me?'

'Anything.'

Jean put her hand over the other woman's. 'Thank you. I know this sounds strange but I'd like you to make me up.'

'Make you up...!' Deepa laughed outright.

'I know, but I'm serious. Make me up so that I look...I mean, I'll never look as beautiful as you, but...'

'Always looking nice, madam.'

'Thank you Deepa, but...well, I hardly ever use make-up. I don't know how to really. Today I want it all. I want to be so that men will stop and look at me – if that's possible with someone like me.'

'Of course possible.' Deepa was regarding her like a mother whose child was about to misbehave. 'But why? Why do you want this?'

'It's just something I want to try.'

'Hm.'

Jean smiled at her. 'You said "anything".'

Deepa still had the old-fashioned look on her face but she said 'If you want, then I will do of course.' She gave Jean another penetrating stare. 'So that men will look at you, yes?'

'Yes.'

They sat together amongst the disconsolate refugees, the children playing and the crying babies, the women bent over cooking stoves. Deepa put a modest store of cosmetics in front of her, but she mixed things creatively and applied them with endless patience. The process seemed to last for ever. Jean sat and received the unfamiliar substances on her face. It was a sensuous experience to feel Deepa's fingers against her skin. The Indian's lovely features were a foot away. Halfway through Deepa stopped and stared into her eyes, in a way she'd never have done during her 'servant' days.

'But *why*?' she said, very seriously.

'You don't want to know.'

'No, no madam, don't do this,' Deepa pleaded. 'Bad idea, madam. Don't do it.'

Jean took Deepa's face in both hands, another gesture that would have been all wrong three months earlier. 'Deepa, my sweet, do I *have* to be "madam"? Don't you think that – as we're just two women travelling so far and enduring so much together, and as I really admire you and I like you so much, and I hope you like me – don't you think you could call me Jean? My name's Jean.'

'Sit still,' Deepa turned her face away in a half-serious display of petulance.

A small mirror was amongst the cosmetic stuff and Jean pointed to it. 'Can I see what I look like?'

'Wait. Wait till I've finished.'

After Deepa handed over the mirror – without a word – she moved away as if uninterested in Jean's reaction.

Jean looked, and cried out in surprise. She looked again. The face that stared back from the glass was one she'd not seen before. The girl-next-door, the healthy outdoors type of woman, that person had vanished. The new one was a creation of enigmatic shadows and shades, someone who looked almost dangerous to know. Jean wasn't at all sure she liked her.

'You *said* so men will admire you,' Deepa threw over her shoulder as she walked off.

There was one nice dress in Jean's rucksack, albeit impossibly creased, and a set of underwear that had always prompted Patrick to jump on her. The river bank afforded no privacy, but as she tried discreetly to put on these garments Deepa came silently forward with a groundsheet to provide cover. She snorted when Jean thanked her.

Footwear was another problem. The utilitarian shoes she wore on the road looked ridiculous against the rest of her kit. Now Deepa approached holding between thumb and forefinger a pair of sandals. They looked a lot better than anything Jean could come up with.

As she prepared to leave, Jyoti ran up, stopped, and stared.

'Jean – is that you?'

'Who me? No, no – I don't know anyone called Jean.'

She'd intended to get a crew member of the 'Flying fish' to fetch the captain, but the man was there on deck again, smoking another cigarette. Perhaps he stood there all the time. She advanced to the edge of the landing-stage and stood staring at him as obviously as she could manage. Once he'd noticed her she communicated in dumb-show, fluttering hands towards her body then raising her (reinforced) eyebrows to convey the idea of a meeting. Her palms were sweating and she half-hoped the captain would ignore her, but he descended the gang-plank at his customary ambling pace. She felt this was a man who would even panic slowly.

He stopped a yard away. 'English?'

'Yes.'

'What do you want?'

'I'd like to speak to you alone.'

'We *are* alone.'

'In your cabin.'

'What do you want?' he repeated, a man of few words.

She approached as close as she dared. I've no idea how to do this, was the thought running through her head; keep eye contact and speak slowly and calmly, like a person who isn't you. 'I want places on the boat,' she said, 'And there's something I'd like to offer you in return. Something I think you would like. Could we talk about it?'

He turned on his heel to go back up the gang-plank. Jean thought she'd lost her chance until a jerk of his head enjoined her to follow.

The cabin was small and reeked of cigarette smoke. A port-hole looked onto the river. A whisky bottle sat on the single chair. She could hardly bring herself to look at the bunk, which displayed some dishevelled and grubby sheets.

In the close surroundings his body smelt sourly of sweat. He turned to face her and for the third time said 'What do you want?'

'I want an agreement with you.'

'What about?'

'I'm with two friends – an Indian woman and her 11-year old child. We need three places on the boat, all the way up-river if possible.'

'For this you buy tickets from the agent on shore.'

'I can't get tickets. I've tried.'

'Then do not waste my time.'

'But I told you – I'm offering something in return.' He didn't react so she took a deep breath and plunged on. 'If you'll allow us on board then...then I'd like to have sex with you.' She said the words but her imagination wouldn't supply the corresponding image, even now standing beside the bunk. She gestured towards it. 'Have sex – you and me.'

There, she'd said it. She felt faint from tension but the Chittagonian's stolid form looked utterly unmoved. She doubted if anything *could* move him. It was a surprise when he spoke.

'You can come. Only you.'

'That's no good. It has to be all three of us.'

'No.'

Jean felt her chance slipping away. 'Maybe I haven't been clear enough,' she said. 'I will give you a really good time. I'll do anything you want.'

'Anything? Do you do...?' He used a term she didn't understand.

'Of course I do that,' she said recklessly. 'What kind of woman do you think I am?'

He stared, and she knew he was on the brink of deciding. But which way? 'Just a minute,' she said. 'It's only fair you should see what you'll be getting.' With difficulty, because her hands were trembling so much, she unbuttoned her dress at the front, all the way down. A breeze wafted through the port-hole to tickle her thighs. There was no point in her trying to adopt a slinky pose – it would have come across as comical – so she stood up straight and stayed still. Even so she felt absurd. She couldn't remember any man but Philip seeing her half-naked before.

'How do I know you will do what you say?' the captain asked eventually.

A wave of relief went through her, mixed with awful trepidation. 'Sir, I'm English. You *know* I will keep my word.' She touched his arm, the most intimate gesture she could manage at that stage. 'You won't be sorry, I promise.'

He grunted, said 'Come on board at mid-day,' and bawled for a crew member to see her to the shore.

Jean returned to the river bank to tell the other two. They said goodbye to Ramesh and his family – though the daughter was unwell – and at twelve precisely the three of them queued amongst dozens of others to get on board. They were in very different states of mind. Jyoti was excited because she'd never been on a paddle-steamer. Jean had willed herself into a state of numbness to exclude thoughts of the future. Deepa had undergone one of the rapid mood changes that Jean was just getting used to. No sign now of her reproachful attitude on the river bank; she stayed by Jean's side, attentive and solicitous.

The ingress of passengers was tightly controlled. Two Burmese policemen were stationed at the top of the gang-plank. One carefully checked tickets or – in Jean's case – reacted to a nod from the captain, lounging nearby. The other policeman monitored the amount of luggage taken on board by each passenger, one bundle per person being the maximum permitted. Jean's party was passed as OK, though they'd loaded Jyoti beyond what she would normally carry. Others were less fortunate. The boat reverberated with wailing passengers whose surplus possessions were hurled unceremoniously into the Irrawaddy. Jean saw a large suitcase submerge in a gurgle of bubbles, followed by a cooking stove. Two umbrellas floated on the surface.

Like others who'd travelled the river before, she knew that people hastened to grab a favourable position on deck. The steamer's layout was similar to ones she'd already seen. The first-class accommodation (which she'd normally have occupied) lay on the forward part of the upper deck, with saloon and dining areas behind them. Otherwise the entire upper space was given over to deck passengers. In the world she'd left behind it would have been unthinkable for an English memsahib to be out on deck but that was where she, Deepa and Jyoti now took up their positions, and in spite of everything she felt profoundly grateful to be there.

There were still a couple of hours to wait, but in mid-afternoon the steamer at last drew away from the river bank amidst the clanging of bells and chatter of passengers – and a greater clamour from those left behind, whose anxieties were all too familiar. The deck where she sat was clogged with refugees. She knew little enough about flotilla customs but reckoned the permitted complement of passengers had been swelled by dozens of 'illegals' like herself. In her imagination the boat sat low in the water and handled sluggishly. Around her was a scene of extraordinary chaos. In the limited space Indian passengers marked out their territory with possessions; rugs, mats, bed rolls, stoves, kettles, and all manner of stuff abounded. People coughed and spat when they felt like it. Men and women alike smoked the famous cheroots, which could be up to a foot long. The chewing of betel nuts was another unsociable habit, since the chewers spat out scarlet streams that stained the deck.

In her relief at being on the move again Jean would have tolerated any number of discomforts. She doubted whether Jyoti was even aware of them. The girl was dazzled by her first experience on the river, her expression alive with interest, her bright eyes flickering in every direction as she absorbed the activity on and off the boat. She jumped for joy as the boat's funnel emitted one of those blasts that newcomers always found so charming.

Jean had a piece of luck. One of the cabins was part-occupied by an official of the Indian Tea Association, who was returning north after what he described as 'this ill-timed visit to Rangoon'. He was Dutch (which meant he spoke excellent English) and – she thought – about 40 years old. An authoritative appearance didn't stand in the way of his very pleasant manner. They exchanged a few words and she introduced him to Deepa and Jyoti. He sat out on deck for a while and soon revealed himself to be very well informed.

'Let's hope the water is deep enough to get us up-river,' he said.

Jean was surprised. 'Is that usually a problem?'

'March is the low-water month. Some days it's OK, some days not.'

'But then how do they know when to make a start?'

'They take soundings up-river in Bhamo and send a daily telegram to the people down here. Usually you need a draught of five feet for a boat that's lightly loaded.'

'But surely this one isn't?' Jean said.

He grinned. 'You spotted that. So...fingers crossed, as you English say.'

The sight of an Englishwoman sitting on the deck affronted the Dutchman and he urged her to take over his cabin berth. Jean was deeply touched but couldn't accept; she'd no intention of separating herself from Deepa and Jyoti.

Amongst other things the man was knowledgeable about the refugee situation further north. She asked how he'd picked up so much information.

'Not as much as before I came south,' he said ruefully. 'Do you know anything about the Indian Tea Association?'

'I'm afraid not,' Jean confessed.

'No reason why you should. It's just that having so many Indian refugees flooding north is causing big problems. Nobody planned for it. How could they?' He gave her a quizzical look. 'For instance I'm sure you three didn't expect to be undertaking this journey.'

'That's an understatement.'

'No, well I don't want to alarm you but conditions up there aren't good. To be frank, a lot of people are dying. It's a tough terrain. There are no proper roads from Burma into India.'

'I don't know if I want to hear this,' said Jean.

'Ah but that's where the Tea Association comes in. Look, I'm a planter. There are dozens like me up there. We've got 600 square miles under tea. I don't want to be immodest but we know the area better than anyone – except the native inhabitants, of course. So the government of India is making use of us. I hope I'm not boring you?'

'Good god no.' She shook her head fiercely.

'I hope not. The point is...'

He broke off as an Indian woman dropped an enormous cheroot which burst into flames – an occasional hazard on the boats. There was a flurry of alarm amongst those sitting nearby. The Dutchman leapt to his feet to stamp it out, and someone else threw a rug over the woman, whose sari was on fire.

'The point is,' her companion continued with scarcely a break, 'The Indian government has realised – *at last* – that they have to help out their own refugees. They've started to do something about it. I don't know which way you intend to go out, but if you do the Kabaw Valley route they're constructing a road between Tamu and Palel.'

'A proper road!'

'Well...let's say it'll be better than it has been. And you'd find Tea Association people along that route setting up camps. With any luck there could be lorries connecting to Imphal and Kohima.'

'But that's wonderful.'

'Steady on now, I don't want to give the impression of a picnic. In fact the Kabaw Valley's a nightmare. But at least something's being done.'

Jean's head was whirling: Tamu...Palel...Imphal...the Kabaw Valley. She had a map in her rucksack and often consulted it, but as yet these were just names.

'Thanks for telling me all this,' she said. 'I'm so horribly ignorant about where you said.'

'Very few people know those places,' he told her. 'And anyway it's wartime. Nobody knows what's going on full stop. Don't just take it from me. Talk to everyone and use your own judgement.'

'Thank you so much. I don't even know your name.'

'I'm Jan.'

'Oh! And I'm Jean, believe it or not!'

'OK Jean. If I hear anything else I'll let you know.'

For several hours the passage up-river was uneventful. In the sunshine the upper deck was warm but not unpleasantly so, and Jean was content to sit and talk and take in the wooded countryside, which she'd not seen before. The water, reddish-brown under the sun, took on a metallic tinge if a cloud came over. She watched the slender egrets negotiating the shallows in their dignified way. When the steamer passed the big lion statues at Kama she felt like disembarking to look around, a throwback to the old touristy days.

In the late afternoon they encountered the problem the Dutchman had alluded to – running aground on a sandbank. She'd heard that steamer captains would move heaven and earth to get off straight away, but this hold-up took ages and required male passengers to climb into small boats before the 'Flying fish' re-floated to a chorus of cheers.

It was dark by the time they'd eaten dinner, prepared jointly by Jean and Deepa. Most unusually, Jyoti said she wasn't hungry. The two women were drinking tea when the moment Jean had tried not to think about arrived. A crew member approached and announced in broken English that the captain wanted to see the English lady. Jean jumped to her feet upsetting a saucepan of water in her nervousness. Immediately Deepa was by her side.

'Don't go,' she whispered. 'He can't do anything.'

'He can put us off the boat,' Jean said. 'But it's not that. I promised him.'

She returned an hour later very different from how she had been before. Her innocence in this situation had been both a blessing and a curse. Jean had not allowed herself to dwell on the forthcoming rendez-vous, but now it was over every feature of the Chittagonian, every clinging iota of his smell and taste seemed to have found its way under her skin, so that it was hard to imagine ever being free of them. Though she tried hard she couldn't shut out the unremitting images of their coupling; she understood that they would never leave her entirely. She didn't once cry over what had happened.

Deepa was ready for her. She had hot water prepared, and an impossibly fragrant soap. Burmese women were accustomed to washing modestly under their lungyis, so passengers saw nothing unusual about Jean undressing beneath a capacious wrap. She felt like a baby as Deepa washed her in the darkness murmuring 'Very sorry madam' and Hindi expressions that sounded like endearments. Jean was glad that Jyoti, flat out on the deck, knew nothing about it. After the cleansing Deepa arranged a comfortable place for her sleep, on mounds of soft clothing, and sat near stroking her face and murmuring over and over in low musical tones. On the river banks the frogs were croaking crazily. The last thing Jean remembered was Deepa's lips on her face.

She woke – not knowing where she was at first – to the unfamiliar motion of the boat and the brightness of early morning on the river; and Deepa, with a cup of hot tea in her hand. She thanked her and hugged her, and would have hugged Jyoti too but the girl looked utterly woebegone, barely stirring from where she lay on deck.

To Jean's surprise she'd woken in quite a composed frame of mind. That her ordeal was over had to be part of it, but there was something else. She was discovering in herself a resilience that she'd been unaware of before the preceding week. Physical stamina, yes, as evidenced by the long-distance cycle rides she used to take around the British countryside, but not the emotional strength that was now making itself felt. That sort of fortitude hadn't been needed in the early years of her marriage and she was surprised and reassured to uncover its existence; and curious to see how far it could take her.

She sat up with a sense of renewed enthusiasm to see what was going on, noticing how busy the river banks were in the early morning. Fishermen were extricating catches from their nets and – in an immemorial tableau – women washed clothes at the water's edge. A posse of bullocks came down to the banks to slurp from the shallows. Every new village passed was an event, with children dancing and shouting and pariah dogs barking as if their lives depended upon it. If she was lucky, she got temple bells as well. At one village she watched a line of *hpongyis*, the Buddhist monks, file out from a monastery in their yellow garbs to receive a free food donation – confirming her view of *hpongyis* as a bunch of sponging free-loaders. When there was nothing to see she was content to sit and be warmed by the sun, with the engines throbbing and the boat making progress northwards.

The peaceful mood ended abruptly when Jyoti rose from the deck and crossed to the gunwales to vomit overboard. Looking absolutely wretched, she asked Deepa to take her to the toilet. The Flying Fish's latrines were not places to linger, but Jyoti visited them four times in the next two hours. On the fourth occasion Jean went with her. There was a queue and Jyoti waited leaning against her, barely able to stand, just about reaching the holes-in-the-ground in time. One look at the watery stuff that poured out of the girl was enough to tell Jean the worst.

Back outside Jyoti almost fell onto the deck. Deepa hovered anxiously.

'What's wrong with me?' the little girl whispered pitifully.

'You're ill,' Jean told her, 'But we're going to get you better. Now think carefully, Jyoti. Back in Prome when we were waiting for a boat, did you eat or drink anything that wasn't prepared by your mother? Maybe your friend's mother gave you something?'

'Yes, I had some soup. And some rice and dahl. Was that bad?'

'Not bad, but perhaps it was that which made you ill.'

'I'm sorry, Jean.'

'No, no, no, my sweet, it's not your fault. Let me talk to your mother for a moment.'

She drew Deepa aside and whispered. 'Keep your voice very low. We don't want people to hear. I'm not sure, but I'm afraid Jyoti has cholera.'

'Oh no! No madam, no.'

'Sshh. She had some food from that Indian family. If they didn't boil things properly...well, that's how the bacteria spreads. Their little girl was ill when we left, wasn't she. Matron warned me there might be cholera in Prome.'

'What can we do?' Deepa's languid manner had quickly unravelled at the news of Jyoti's sickness. 'Is it bad?'

'It will be if we can't deal with it. Cholera's very serious.' She looked helplessly around the crowded boat. 'And this is the last place you'd want to get it.'

'What can I do?' Deepa said. 'I must do something.'

'I know.' Jean squeezed her hand. 'Let me think.' She gazed across the deck, thronged with people, and beyond it to the river bank and a rudimentary village that had just come into view. One peep about cholera to the steamer's crew and they'd be put ashore into just such a setting, where Jyoti's chances would be zero. 'No-one must know about this,' she whispered, 'Or they'll throw us off the boat – and I wouldn't blame them. There is something you can do, Deepa, and that's keep boiling up water. As soon as you've boiled one lot, start another, and keep doing it.'

'Of course.' Deepa immediately knelt to get the stove alight. 'Why do this?'

'Sshh. Because the diarrhoea will go on and on. It'll get worse. With all this liquid going out of her body we have to replace it. Do we have any salt?'

'We have salt.'

'OK, so put a teaspoon into each mug of water that she drinks. It's probably not the right proportion but it'll help. We have to persuade Jyoti to keep drinking, though she won't feel like it.'

'She'll do it. She's a good girl.'

'She's a wonderful girl. Oh this is so unfair.' Again Jean scanned the deck anxiously. 'There's one big problem.'

'What?'

'With cholera you need almost permanent access to a toilet. And here on the boat people have to queue. It's not going to work.'

They were interrupted by the Dutchman, who'd materialised from nowhere. 'Will you forgive me?' he said to Deepa. 'I'd like to talk to Jean in my cabin.'

The cabin was no bigger than the captain's, but in a more hygienic condition. The Dutchman introduced his room-mate, a French colleague called Pierre, another planter.

'I'm sorry Jean,' he said, 'But I couldn't help noticing you have a problem.'

Jean hung her head. 'You know, then?'

'I think so. I've seen cholera before.'

'I realise I'm putting everyone at risk. We ought to be put ashore. But then...I haven't told Deepa this, but then Jyoti would die.'

'Do not go ashore. You know, this cabin has a toilet. Pierre and I have talked it over and we want to repeat the offer that you move into the cabin, all three of you. And this time I really must insist.'

At this juncture kindness was the one thing Jean couldn't withstand. She stood before him helplessly making little honking sounds.

The Dutchman grinned. 'We'll take that as a yes.'

The two men had already packed their belongings into cases, which Pierre now carried outside. Jean threw a tear-stained 'thank you' after him.

'If you keep your little girl in here,' the Dutchman went on, you won't need to worry about infecting anyone else. But if you don't mind me asking, do you have any plans to get her back to health?'

'Apart from replacing the liquid she loses...well, I need to get her to a decent hospital. There is a vaccine – antibiotics – but god knows where I'd find it.'

'Something I heard may help,' he said, 'If you can keep her stable as far as Yenangyaung. That would be a night or two I should think.'

'But will there be a good hospital there?'

'Probably not, given the state the country is in, but there could be something better. You know about the Glosters — the garrison from Rangoon?'

Jean stared. 'Yes of course. My husband was with them.'

'There you are then. What I heard was that they're being pulled back to garrison Yenangyaung. Not sure, but it sounded genuine. The military would have medical facilities for sure.'

She stepped forward and took one of his hands in both hers. 'Who sent you, Jan? Are you an angel?'

He grinned again, and took a couple of steps to the door. 'I'm a planter. Now if you need me, you know I won't have gone far.'

For the next day and a half she and Deepa stayed in the cabin trying to keep Jyoti as stable as possible. They ate there and slept there and carried Jyoti in and out of the toilet. The room stank but they didn't care. Jean warned Deepa not to put anything near her mouth that might conceivably carry the infection. Matron's 'other bits and pieces' in the medical kit didn't include antibiotics, unfortunately, but there were some pain-killers and a bottle of tonic, which helped a little. Even so Jyoti's condition grew worse, and there were times when the girl hardly knew where she was. She was never less than an exemplary patient, drinking whenever it was required and not once complaining. Deepa watched her every move and hardly slept for two nights in a row.

Early on the third morning the Dutchman knocked on the door to report that the boat was pulling into Yenangyaung. Shortly afterwards they half-carried Jyoti out on deck.  They were faced with an extraordinary landscape, as if they'd moved from the earth to the surface of the moon.

## ~ Six ~

### Oil town sojourn

When Jean helped Jyoti onto the jetty at Yenangyaung the first thing that struck her was the heat, much more extreme than it had been further south.  She'd known they were approaching Burma's hottest month of the year, but it was still a shock to be abruptly exposed to 100 degrees – plus the direct glare of the sun.

The second shock was the Yenangyaung landscape.  The scenery they'd passed through since leaving Prome had been undeniably pretty. Now, emerging from the cabin after a night's travel, she found everything transformed. Jean had never seen oil wells before and the array of steel derricks towering above was an awesome spectacle. And the land had changed too. The picturesque greenery of the riverside had given way to a scorched dust-bowl dotted with thorn bushes. It was as if someone had waved a giant blow-torch to fashion a desert. What also struck Jean, coming from a boat bursting at the seams with people, was Yenangyaung's emptiness. Here was a town that had clearly housed a sizeable population yet now showed little sign of life; just the water, the deserted river banks, and the giant derricks in the sky.

After dropping the three of them off, the 'Flying fish' remained moored to the jetty. No-one else left the boat, and it looked as if the Chittagonian captain hoped to stock up on supplies. Some Indians who'd been loitering nearby slouched across and talked to members of the crew. There was no-one else around; not one person for Jean and Deepa to talk to.

A row of smart-looking bungalows was visible on a rise high above the Irrawaddy, with a steep path leading from it towards the jetty. As Jean looked round she spotted a substantial figure in khaki shorts and shirt moving down the incline towards them. As it came closer she gave a gasp of pleasure. She recognised this man – Sergeant Johnson of the Glosters. He was rolling rather than walking down the slope, perspiring freely and grinning. She remembered Philip and herself laughing at the notion of Johnson charging the Japanese with fixed bayonet. Well, she wasn't laughing now. She felt tremendously happy to see him. And the

Dutchman had been right; the Glosters *were* in town.

'Mrs Costain,' Johnson gasped, lurching up out of breath. 'What a very pleasant surprise.'

'And how wonderful to see you, sergeant.' She discarded all semblance of military discipline and leant up to kiss him. 'Meet my friend Deepa.'

Johnson shook hands with Deepa and for good measure raised his cap. His stomach was wobbling like a jelly that had been made up with too much water. 'And who have we got here?' he said, pointing at the wilting figure of Jyoti.

'This is Deepa's daughter, Jyoti.' Jean closed upon Johnson to whisper in his ear. 'I think Jyoti has contracted cholera. I'm pretty sure of it. She's got all the symptoms.'

Johnson nodded. 'Then I'll get the doctor straight away, Mrs Costain.'

'Thank you, sergeant. Thank you so much. And do you happen know if there's anywhere we might stay until Jyoti recovers?'

'Somewhere to stay? How many bedrooms would you like? With garden or without?'

'I don't understand.'

'Sorry, Mrs – just pulling your leg. We've got bungalows coming out of our ears. What's today – March the 16th if I'm not mistaken. Four days ago they evacuated the women and children on steamers up-river. Some of the oil people have left too. So you see, loads of properties are available. I'll show you one if you'll just follow me.' He bent down and picked up Jyoti as if she were a feather duster. 'If you don't mind, young miss, I'll give you a lift.'

Jean put up a warning hand and did some more whispering. 'Do be careful, Sergeant. Jyoti will be highly infectious.'

'Now don't you worry, Mrs Costain. We've all had our jabs for cholera – and a lot else besides. I felt like a pin-cushion at the time.'

When they'd laboured up the slope Johnson led them to a 3-bedroom bungalow. 'If you don't like this one...' he began.

'Oh it's fine,' Jean told him. 'Compared to what we're used to, this is a palace.'

'In that case I'll go and find the doctor.'

'There's just one thing, sergeant. Do you know what happened to Philip?'

'Now there's a question.' Johnson had an odd look on his face. 'I'll try and get back to you on that as soon as possible.'

They put Jyoti straight to bed, then investigated the bungalow. Moving into someone else's home was a strange experience, because the former tenants' possessions were all around them. It was clear that the call to evacuate had come through suddenly, and that a stringent limit had been placed upon luggage. (Jean recalled the policeman on the *Flying fish* hurling excess luggage into the Irrawaddy.) The bungalow appeared to have been occupied by a family with two children, because two of the bedrooms had toys crammed onto shelves, and even on the floor as if their offspring were called away in the middle of playing. The other rooms conveyed a similar sense of intimacy. There were books in bookcases and pictures on the walls. In the kitchen, crockery had been set out to dry on the draining board. A working short-wave radio stood on the table.

After five minutes the Glosters' doctor arrived and went straight in to examine Jyoti. He was there quite some time and emerged poker-faced to report.

'I'm afraid your daughter is seriously ill,' he told Deepa. 'To be frank, you've done well to keep her alive, but the impact of cholera on an 11-year old, in those circumstances...well, it can't be good.'

'But she'll be OK, won't she?' Jean said.

The man pursed his lips. Jean was quick to recognise the gesture: a medical man prevaricating over bad news. 'I've given her an injection of vaccine. We should see the results very quickly. Keep her drinking – boiled water, of course – and put these into it.' He held out a small carton. 'The instructions are inside. I'll come back this evening – say, at six. And I'll bring doses of vaccine for both of you.'

At the door, seeing him out, Jean said 'I'm a nurse, doctor. Please tell me – are you very concerned about Jyoti?'

He regarded her – deciding whether to tell the truth, Jean thought. 'I think we can control the cholera now,' he said. 'It's the effect upon such a young child that concerns me. I won't pretend it'll be easy. It's a pity these bungalows are so hot in the summer months. If she survives, there'll be a long period of recuperation. On no account should the girl be moved.'

'We won't need to move her, will we? I mean, the Japanese aren't on the door-step?'

'You'll need to talk to the soldier boys about that. But no, we should be all right here for a while yet.'

When he'd gone she took Deepa in her arms and held on. Deepa was never a drama queen and there were rarely tears, but she was naturally very upset. Jean felt in quite a state herself. In the middle of their embrace someone rapped on the door. Jean went to open it.

'Philip!' She was literally open-mouthed. 'You're here!'

'Not unwelcome, I hope.'

She gulped. 'Sorry – I didn't know.'

'Surely Johnson told you?'

'No, I...'

'Didn't he! I'll have his guts for garters.'

'Don't do that. It was just his little joke. I think he was trying to give me a surprise.' She remembered that this was her husband and stepped up to kiss his cheek. When he put his arms round her it felt odd, so soon after Deepa's embrace. And when she – belatedly – asked him in, there was a sense of his invading her space, though it was space she'd only just occupied herself.

They went through into the kitchen, where Deepa tactfully made way for them. Philip gave the Indian woman a nod, but nothing more.

Jean made a conscious effort to get a conversation going. 'This is so unexpected, Philip.'

'Are you pleased to see me?'

'I'm relieved you're safe, of course I am. Anything could have happened. The last I knew you were leaving Rangoon by sea – you and your last-ditchers. '

'Yes, that didn't work out,' he said ruefully. 'Those boats were impossibly overcrowded. We ended up driving along the Prome Road.'

She looked up sharply. 'Then you went the same way as us!'

'Except by the time we got onto it the Japs had set up a road block. Loads of British troops got stuck there.'

'So how...?'

'You wouldn't credit it, Jean. The Japs diverted to Rangoon instead.

For them that was the big prize – and we'd already given it up. That allowed us to go on to Prome – and beyond.'

'Beyond...you mean on the river?'

'No, we stayed with the jeep. There's a sort of track along the river bank. Only got here three days ago.'

Jean had found some tea-bags belonging to the previous tenants, and she boiled the kettle to make two cuppas. She felt comfortable keeping the conversation to military matters, but of course the personal stuff soon stuck its head in.

'We need to talk, Jean.'

'I suppose.'

'Of course we do. It's daft, having everything up in the air like this.'

'Is it?' She shrugged. 'Isn't everyone up in the air?'

'Look, there've always been two clubs in Yenangyaung – British and American – and believe it or not the British Club's still open. Why don't we go there this evening? We could have a drink...something to eat. How about it?'

'Are you asking me out, Philip Costain?'

'Yes.' He grinned and looked defiant. 'Yes I am, dammit. Don't tell me you're washing your hair tonight.'

'I think I'd *better* wash it, if you're going to be seen with me.'

'Is that a yes, then?'

'OK, it's a date.' She remembered the doctor was coming at 6.30. 'Say 7.30?'

'I'll call for you then. It's wonderful to see you again.'

With Jyoti so sick, Deepa wouldn't leave the bungalow, but after resting for a couple of hours Jean went out to have a look round.

Courtesy – once again – of the former tenants, she took a parasol as protection against the burning sun. Even so she was sweating profusely after five minutes in the open.

Yenangyaung was one of the most extraordinary places she'd ever seen. She walked further than intended looking for its centre which didn't seem to exist. In a sense, she came to realise, the power station *was* the centre, the reason for the town's existence. Beyond that were the well-appointed bungalows for all the oil people; and then – the engine of their social life – the British Club, with its empty tennis courts and the pool and a few men splashing up and down in the water. Two of them made a point of paddling to the side to say hello, and it occurred to her that amongst the handful of people she'd seen since arriving, not one had been a woman. At this juncture in the town's history she was a rare commodity.

She couldn't imagine living in Yenangyaung, even when it was firing on all cylinders. Rangoon's social life had had its limitations, but the capital was a far bigger and more diverse place than this one-horse, one-industry location stranded miles from anywhere, fringed by dozens of Eiffel Tower lookalikes and desert scenery, the only green coming from the manicured lawns of posh bungalows.

While out, she managed to buy some food for Deepa to eat that evening. Later Philip arrived with military precision at the appointed time and took her away.

The British Club's facilities were arranged round the pool, with places to sit outside and in. They chose to go in to escape the mosquitoes. There were dozens of people around, almost exclusively off-duty military and oil company employees. Jean was one of three women present, all of them attracting attention. She could have got blind drunk on the drinks men offered to buy her, especially when Philip's back was turned. She yielded to a gin and tonic that he ordered at the bar. A gin and tonic! If felt as if she'd stepped back to another age.

Philip had reserved a table in the food area, and they made their way across to it. Sergeant Johnson was at another table cradling a pint glass; he gave her a little wave when Philip's attention was elsewhere. As they sat down, Jean ordered egg and chips.

'So many people,' she said, waving at the room. 'When I walked round the town this afternoon it seemed deserted.'

'I think most people who still live here use the club,' Philip said. 'A hundred and eighty Glosters for a start.'

'Have you lost many men?' she asked.

He shook his head. 'We've been fortunate so far. Unlike some other units. The poor devils at the Sittaing, for instance. Hundreds are missing. And with the Japs, "missing" can mean anything – dead, wounded, captured, drowned, beheaded, crucified...'

She shivered. 'Don't.'

The waiter came back with their orders. This was amazing, Jean thought. You ask for food and a few minutes later the stuff turns up; a life-style she'd almost forgotten about. She didn't demur when Philip ordered her another gin and tonic.

'What are you plans, Jean?' he said. 'I assume you won't stick around here very long.'

'Actually we will be here a while. Jyoti's very ill with cholera. She can't be moved.'

'*She* can't,' he said meaningfully.

'Let's not go there again, Philip. When it's time to move the three of us will go together.' He said nothing, though she knew what he was thinking. 'Anyway, Yenangyaung's not at risk, is it?' She looked round the room, which was still heaving with people. 'All these oil people are still here.'

'They're here because the British army needs oil. Doesn't mean they'll stay for ever.' He lowered his voice. 'Don't repeat this to anyone, but there's a demolition team in town. If need be the whole place will go up in smoke.'

She interrupted her eating to work out the implications of this. 'But...the Japanese aren't this far north...are they?'

'They're on the way. Oh, we're supposed to stop them all right. That's all London talks about. But then they've not seen our troops. We fulfil a long-standing British tradition of being unprepared at the beginning of a war. Will the Japs reach Yenangyaung? I really don't know. They need oil too, you know. And if they take control of the air, well... Talking of that, did you see any Jap aircraft on the way here?'

'One plane. On the Prome Road.'

'And on the river?'

'No, nothing.'

'Hmm.' He pursed his lips in a familiar gesture. 'That may not last. If they drive the RAF out of Magwe...'

The second gin was making her head swim. 'Why don't *you* take over the Burma operations?' she said gaily. 'You're really good at anticipating what will happen.'

He breathed on his fist and polished an imaginary decoration. 'I think I'm a bit young for that. Actually there's a new general here. Chap called Slim.'

'Slim?'

'Bill Slim. He's supposed to be good.'

'Well make sure you get to talk to him. Then he can promote you.'

He smiled for the first time since they'd met up again. 'Thank you, my loyal wife. I've got a good brain, I think, but I'm not so good with people...as you know.'

'You're all right,' she said, and – fuelled by the gin – covered his hand with hers.

Philip was quick to respond. 'You look nice this evening.'

Jean cursed herself silently. She'd resolved to keep the evening light-hearted, but drink had undone her. 'You know what I'm wearing?' she said, trying to retrieve the situation. 'This dress belonged to the woman who had the bungalow I'm staying in. I've just nicked it from the wardrobe.'

She was too late. He'd already adopted a more intimate tone of voice. Only Philip would attempt seduction over egg and chips. 'Where I'm staying,' he said, 'I've got the place to myself. You could call in. Stay, if you like...'

She felt a flush spread across her face and knew she'd turned bright red. 'Better not,' she stammered. 'I'm sorry, Philip. I don't want to leave Deepa alone with Jyoti so ill, and...oh, I don't know, it's the war...everything's so complicated and uncertain. I'm sorry, Philip.'

'OK,' he said, but the evening was spoilt, and before long he drove her back to the bungalow. They separated at the front door.

'Thank you so much,' she told him.

'Let me know if you need anything,' were his parting words.

Over the next three weeks she saw little of her husband. He was busy, but he was also hurt by her rejection of him. He ate at the British Club, mostly alone, and Jean had meals with Jyoti in the bungalow. Both women were absorbed by Jyoti's condition. The outward symptoms of cholera were under control, but as the doctor had foretold her young body couldn't handle the side-effects. After three days he warned Deepa to expect the worst. There was little either of the women could do except sit by the girl's bed pressing cold cloths to her head to alleviate the stifling heat – and encouraging her to eat and drink something. Then when Jyoti appeared at last to have overcome the effects of cholera the doctor announced that she'd contracted pneumonia, and they entered a new spell of treatment. Deepa herself looked ill from worrying. Jean was more affected than she'd ever have thought possible. She'd no children of her own – hadn't thought of having any – but over the past few weeks Jyoti's personality had wormed its way into her affections. She knew the girl's death would deal a devastating blow to them both.

Jean would never have credited it but the turning point seemed to revolve around a teddy bear. She'd been vaguely aware that the bear was amongst the toys scattered around the bedroom – to be precise, sitting up stiffly with its back against the wall. Some ten days after their arrival in Yenangyaung they noticed it was on Jyoti's pillow. Neither of them saw how it got there, but they concluded that the girl had left her bed during the night and claimed the creature. It was, Deepa confirmed, the only toy Jyoti had, the others having been left in Rangoon.

It was an odd thing for Jyoti to choose. She'd overlooked some more respectable 'teddies' that were sitting in a row on a cupboard shelf. The bear was a more dubious proposition. He was covered in an unusual, threadbare material, dirty yellow in colour, and the ends of his arms and legs were patched by what had obviously been the toes of nylon stockings. The eyes, nose and mouth were sewn in black wool, the mouth unevenly, so that the creature appeared to be leering.

'And who's this?' Jean asked Jyoti, the first time she saw it on the pillow.

'It's a friend,' Jyoti said.

'A friend, eh! Does it have a name?'

'A sort of name. He's "bear".'

Jean laughed. 'Is that a name?'

'Not really. I may think of one later. Do you like him?'

She inspected him critically. 'He looks very reliable – and that's the most important thing you want in a friend.'

Maybe it was Jean's imagination, but she felt a glimmer had returned to Jyoti's eyes; an echo, at least, of that special animation that informed the girl's face. In any case she dated the start of the recovery from the day the odd-looking animal arrived. Even the doctor said the patient looked better – in his case without ascribing any credit to the bear.

On one of the man's daily visits Jean consulted him about her own health. She was concerned lest the encounter with the steamer captain had given her a disease, though she hardly knew enough about such matters to frame the right question. The doctor checked her over and said she seemed OK – 'Most of the sexually-transmitted diseases would have come through by now if they were going to' – but he urged her to have a blood test in India to check for syphilis. There she had to leave it.

Jean had been in Yenangyaung for over three weeks before she sat down again in the company of her husband. No cheery British Club this time; it had been shut down as the number of expatriates in town gradually dwindled away. Instead Philip sent a message via Sergeant Johnson that he would call at the bungalow the following morning to discuss a matter of urgency. He turned up dead on time, as usual. Jean showed him into the kitchen and made them both cups of tea. Deepa had gone out to buy food and Jyoti was playing in her bedroom, looking – at last – much more like her usual self. Her recovery, when it came, had been rapid.

Jean waved Philip into a kitchen chair. They were ill at ease with each other, not surprisingly as she'd hardly thrown more than a 'hello' in his direction for the past fortnight.

'Well, what is it, Philip?' she said.

'I wanted to put you in the picture.'

'That's good of you. I know how busy you are. Johnson said you were working all hours.'

'A case of having to. Now look, Jean,' he burst out with sudden irritation, 'You've got to get out of Yenangyaung. It's ridiculous that you're still around.'

'As it happens, Jyoti is just about well enough to travel now. What's the problem?'

'Where do I start. Everything's kicking off. We've just heard the latest. British troops are on the way here – moving up the east bank of the river.'

'But that's good!'

'No, because the Japs are here too. There's going to be one hell of a fight – and I don't give much for our chances. They've got complete control of the air. It'll be a long while before you see another British plane, that's for sure.'

'Then why...' She always hesitated to ask about military tactics for fear of looking stupid. 'Then why haven't they bombed us already?'

'Why do you think? They want the oil.'

'Oh, of course.'

'But they're not going to get it, are they. The demolition squad goes into action in two days time. Then the balloon really goes up. You must get away.'

She made up her mind. 'All right, I'll talk to Deepa. Maybe we'll leave the day after tomorrow. Thanks for telling me, Philip. Is there any chance we can get a steamer up-river?'

'No, no, no – you've left it too late for that.' He was losing his rag again. 'Now look, I'll be moving out too before long. I could find you a place in my jeep. I shouldn't, but I will.'

'And the others – Deepa and Jyoti?'

'You know I can't do that.'

'Then we'll have to take our chances,' she said firmly.

He got abruptly to his feet, but she forestalled him. 'Please Philip, help me. What's our best way out of the country? You know the picture as well as anyone.'

He huffed and puffed, but sat down again. 'Nobody knows, that's the trouble. Especially now. I hate to offer advice. I may be sending you to your death.'

'Something Philip, *please*. Anything.'

He glared at her. 'Give me a sheet of paper.'

She pushed a notepad across the table and he took a pencil from his pocket and sketched a very rough map of Burma. 'I'd say you have two lousy options, god help you. There's still an airport operational at Myitkyina, in the north. I hear the Governor's intending to fly out from there – a rat abandoning the sinking ship. A rail line goes up to it from near Mandalay, but it may or may not be open. Mandalay was bombed to smithereens on Good Friday. Thousands died.'

'How awful.'

'Yes, Jean. It's called war. People get killed.' He reined himself in again, unusually tentative. 'I don't know about Myitkyina. From what I hear there are thousands waiting for flights. They're loading up Douglas transports with 75 refugees a time but...' He shook his head. 'I just don't know.'

'And the other option?'

'You keep to the India side. Try and get onto the river Chindwin further up. There should be boats. It's navigable as far as Kalewa. Then you walk, making for Tamu and Palel. A hell of a walk.'

She remembered what the Dutchman had told her. 'But the Indian government's building a road there.'

'That's right!' He was always astonished if she had up-to-date information. 'That would help – *if* you can get that far. The Kalewa route goes through the Kabaw Valley – a hundred miles of it.'

The name sounded familiar. 'Is that bad?' she asked.

'I'm afraid so. It's one of the most unhealthy places in the world. Malaria. Damn great mosquitoes. Famous for them. It's not good news, Jean.'

Now she remembered. The Dutchman on the boat had talked about the Kabaw Valley. No-one seemed very fond of the place. She drew a deep breath. 'Well...it can't be helped. We'll have to try. I've got a supply of Mecrapine.'

He nodded. 'That makes a difference. Anyway...don't know why I'm painting such a black picture. I'll probably end up in the Kabaw Valley myself.'

'You're kidding, aren't you.' She gave him a hard look. 'I mean, the army's staying put, surely? They won't abandon Burma.'

He shrugged. 'Do you want to bet? We've done nothing but retreat so far.'

'But...'

'I don't have a clue, Jean. None of us do. Look, let me know when you've decided...when you're going to leave. You'll need help to get onto the right road. I'll send Johnson to walk you down there. He seems to like you.' He got to his feet awkwardly. 'So...I'll say goodbye now. Easier that way.'

She stood too. 'Thanks for your help, Philip. I'm sorry I've messed everything up, but...oh, it's been an impossible situation.'

'It's all right. It's not your fault. Everything's up the creek.' He took her hand in an oddly formal gesture.

'Thanks for looking after me. I appreciate it.'

She talked to Deepa that afternoon and they agreed to leave in two days. It gave them time to boil up a whole load of rice for the journey. They agonised over what to pack, keeping it down to a bare minimum – food, water, ground-sheets, a change of clothes – split between the two of them. Jean relayed what Philip had said about the Kabaw Valley and handed over two-thirds of the Mecrapine.

'Don't forget,' she urged, 'One every day for each of you.'

They decided Jyoti would carry nothing until they were sure of her strength, but the girl had other ideas. 'I'll carry Bear,' she told them.

Deepa said something to her in Hindi. Jyoti never had tantrums, but she immediately went very quiet.

'What did you tell her?' Jean asked.

'I said the bear not hers, madam. Belonging to children from the bungalow.'

'Oh but that's...' Jean began, and then stopped, not wanting to come between mother and child. 'You know Deepa, anything could happen,' she went on after a minute or two. 'The Japanese could come here and take everything. Or they could bomb the place to pieces.'

Deepa gave one of her looks.

'*One* bear?' Jean said, in a quiet, coaxing way. 'That wouldn't hurt, surely?'

'This is *your* wish, then,' Deepa said, making as if to flounce away. '*Your* fault. Bad madam. Bad, stealing person.'

She said something to Jyoti in Hindi, and Jean loved the expression that registered on the girl's face. Later Deepa found a small shoulder bag so that her daughter could carry Bear in comfort.

Sergeant Johnson turned up at 10am on the day they'd agreed. Even at that early hour the sun was ferocious.

'Everything ship-shape and correct, ladies?' he enquired, standing massively on the thresh-hold.

He presented Jyoti with a bag of liquorice all-sorts, obtained by some sleight-of-hand that all soldiers were proficient in. 'Could've got you a chocolate bar,' he told her, 'But they just melt.'

They walked away from the bungalow leaving the door unlocked. Johnson offered to carry things, but Jean said they must get used to their loads straight away. They made an odd quartet – the two women, a young girl, and a large soldier. Despite his great bulk Johnson moved steadily forward with an ambling gait. Jean said she was sorry they'd obliged him to walk so far in the heat.

'Don't you worry, Mrs Costain,' he replied, 'I maybe could lose a touch of weight off the hips.' He nodded in the direction of Jyoti, who was striding out beside them. 'Young miss seems to be goin' well.'

'Thank goodness,' Jean said.

'Reckon it'll take half hour to reach the road,' Johnson said.

'And do you think we'll be able to keep to it, Sergeant?' Jean asked. 'I mean, would it be easy to get lost?'

'Don't think so, Mrs. There'll be plenty of refugees goin' same way.'

'Oh, I see.'

'An' more than that, I reckon you'll see some of us sooner or later.'

'What, the army!'

'Could be. We've had reports. 1st Burma division and 17th Indian heading up beside the river. Can't see what other way they'd go.'

They were out of Yenangyaung's environs now and into the absurd surrounding landscape, one empty yellowing ridge after another. Passing a thorn bush was an event.

'What we *don't* want to see is the Japs,' Johnson said.

Jean looked across, alarmed. 'Do you think that's possible?'

'They're 'ere, Mrs. They're everywhere.'

Jyoti piped up in her precise treble voice. 'What are the Japanese like, Mr Johnson?'

'Oh they're an 'orrible sight, miss. Nasty little people 'bout three foot high, come up to your shoulder, maybe. 'Orrible yeller colour, bit like the ground we're walkin' on. Not to be confused with the Chinese, now. They're round about an'all.'

'What are the Chinese like?' Jyoti said.

'Just the same, miss, cept they're on our side. Least, we think they are. They don't like the Japs, anyway. They don't like the Japs a whole lot more than we don't like 'em.' He slowed his pace for a moment, having outlined the international situation. 'There you are, miss. Now you know everything I know.'

## ~ Seven ~
## The battle of Yenangyaung

Johnson's estimate of half an hour to reach the road had been spot on, but in other respects he'd not fully anticipated events. Once they'd left the town, the little party of four plodded in silence through the desolate landscape, crossing one ridge then another, always with more ridges before them, and nothing but the ranks of steel derricks towering behind and the unreal sun above.

Within seconds it all changed. They breasted yet another mound and saw before them more action than they'd experienced in the past month. Jean was gob-smacked. The road was there all right, stretching as far as the eye could see, but so too was a military panorama crawling along it, an interminable, twisting ribbon of men and machines: motorised transports in the form of lorries, trucks, ambulances, jeeps, tanks; homespun carts drawn by bullocks or mules, with Indian drivers perched on top; Sikhs on scrawny horses, rifles across their knees; and hundreds of men on foot lugging packs and rifles or prodding into action heavily-laden mules. Thick dust churned up by this cavalcade clogged the stifling air, which reverberated with the harsh braying of the mules.

'Gor-blimey,' exclaimed Sergeant Johnson, 'Gor-bleedin'-blimey,' before – recalling the more decorous front he presented to the female sex – he added 'Beggin' your presence, ladies'.

Jyoti, wide-eyed with excitement, was virtually dancing on the spot, but Jean's thoughts were more calculating. She could see clusters of Indian refugees down there, shoved to the side of the road by the military, and her preoccupations were 'Now what? Where do *we* stand amongst this lot? Where will refugees come in the pecking order?'

They said goodbye to Sergeant Johnson on top of the mound. Jean thanked him warmly and stood on tip-toe to bestow a kiss.

'Very good luck, ladies,' he said. 'You deserve to get back safely.'

Watching his hour-glass figure shuffling back toward Yenangyaung, she felt a pang. She, Deepa and Jyoti had been safely housed and guarded by the Glosters for a whole month, but not any more; they were on their own again.

On their own, that is, with hundreds of British soldiers. They scrambled down the ridge towards the traffic. Once she was nearer Jean saw the awful state of the men: bearded faces, red-rimmed eyes staring straight ahead, khaki shirts stained white from dried sweat. They looked as if they'd travelled non-stop for hours. She knew it was 115 degrees in the shade and there was no shade, so no need to tell her that heat and thirst were the enemies, with hunger a poor third. When had these men last drunk anything at all, she thought, seeing the empty water-bags banging against their hips. Dust had settled on their faces, giving the soldiers a spectral appearance.

A cart containing a dozen men moved sedately towards them, drawn by two bullocks. As she watched, a young officer jumped from it and ran towards a clapped-out jeep abandoned by the road-side. He carried several empty water-bags in his arms, and in a trice was kneeling by the vehicle to fiddle under the radiator, one of the bags held in place beneath it. A chorus of groans came from his comrades as the radiator yielded, at best, a few drops of rusty water. The young officer scrambled to his feet and caught Jean's eye.

'Damn all there.'

'What a pity,' Jean said. 'Would it really have been drinkable?'

'Better than nothing. No anti-freeze, anyway.'

She laughed, and so did he. His face was as ravaged as anyone's, but the eyes looked remarkably clear and positive.

'Are you English?' His surprise registered clearly, though the voice – emerging from lips that were cracked and bleeding – was little more than a croak.

'Military wife,' she said, 'On the run with my two friends here.'

He waved to Deepa and Jyoti.

Jean was surprised by her next action, because it contradicted all her carefully nurtured rules of survival. She held out own water-bag. 'Have a drink, why don't you.'

He grinned and shook his head. 'I couldn't do that.'

'Go on,' she urged. 'Treat yourself to a mouthful at least. I'd like you to.'

He fixed the eyes on her again, then accepted the water-bag and took a single modest swallow. A volley of outraged 'heys' came from his mates in the cart. He stood for a moment savouring the unaccustomed sensation of water in his throat.

'Will you marry me?' he said.

She laughed. 'It's tempting, but I'd have to dispose of that husband I mentioned.'

'Oh well.' He looked up at the cart, now 20 yards down the road, and held out a hand. 'Better rejoin my unit, I suppose. I'm Bruce.'

They shook hands. 'I'm Jean.'

He walked a few paces, then turned back. 'Look, would you like a lift?'

Jean was completely taken aback. 'What?'

'In the cart. It beats walking in this heat.'

'Are you kidding? There are three of us.'

'I know that.' He grinned again; he was always grinning.

'But would there be room?'

'Oh the blokes'll shove up. They'd appreciate some female company. The only downside — I ought to mention it — is you could be shot at. We're bound to get into some fighting here. If the Japs are aiming at us...well, you could buy it instead.'

She had a word with Deepa, then turned back to him. 'We'd get it anyway, if there are shells flying about.'

'That's true. Come on then.' He bellowed down the road. 'Hey you lot, wait for us.'

They soon caught up with the cart. Bruce got in first, then helped the other three. Jyoti was lifted in bodily. Deepa put one foot onto the running board and went over the side as gracefully as she did everything else. Jean followed, except that boarding somehow involved Bruce putting an arm round her waist and her seeming to enjoy it. She ignored the meaningful look from Deepa; the woman never missed anything.

They settled down on the cart's wooden boards with their backs against the raised side. If not exactly comfortable it was a sight better than trudging along the road-side covered in dust – the fate of the Indian refugees they now passed along the way. Like Deepa, Jean had covered up against the sun, wearing long sleeves and something over her head. Even so she could feel the heat burning her neck and shoulders through the material of her blouse.

The cart's Indian driver encouraged the two bullocks with guttural cries like 'Jor se challo', which Deepa translated as 'Get a move on'. The animals' jerky motion took some getting used to. Jean had once been on a camel, and recognised certain similarities. Bruce nodded towards them as they lurched onwards, heads bobbing.

'Funny creatures.'

'Don't you like them?' Jean said.

'You get to like the pace. It's how life should be. They take some getting used to though. We tended to overload them at first. Got the hang of it now.  And if we hit sand – you may see this – well, a lorry will get stuck, likely as not, but the good old bullocks keep on going.'

On went the cavalcade at the same steady pace.  Bruce introduced the men, who were unresentful about the invasion of their space and eager to engage their new companions in conversation.  Jyoti entered into an intense discussion about mules with one of them.  There was plenty of good-natured teasing.  Jean felt enormous sympathy for these soldiers.  She'd at least come from comfortable surroundings armed with a full water-bag.  They'd been travelling for days on minimum provisions.  Most of them looked close to the edge.

One slightly-built young chap had a broken arm in plaster and suffered at every lurch of the cart.  She went across to him on her knees.

'Forgive the intrusion, but I'm a nurse.  That arm's painful, isn't it?'

'It's all right miss.  I'll be OK.'

'May I make a suggestion?  It'll hurt less if we strap the arm to your chest, so it can't move about.  That's the usual procedure.'

A strap was found and the bad arm bound up, giving the man immediate relief.  Now that Jean's nursing credentials had been demonstrated, others came forward with problems sustained in action. She managed to help some of them, using the unit's medical kit.  For good measure Deepa produced from her bag a lip salve, which was circulated to address the cracked-lips problem that affected nearly everyone.

At mid-day the men had some lunch.  They called it that, though the food on offer struck Jean as risible – in effect, biscuits with a smear of paste added, washed down with a quick swallow of water.  The lunch situation was a source of mild embarrassment. The men offered their food and water round. The women had their own – more acceptable provisions – but not enough for *them* to offer to a dozen people. No-one took offence, but Jean wasn't happy with the outcome and resolved to seek a different way of handling the next meal.

As they ate, a single Japanese plane turned up and circled around them. She could easily imagine it swooping down, guns blazing, and felt their vulnerability in the open cart. Bruce seemed less concerned.

'It's on reconnaissance,' he told her. 'He's not the first.'

'And if they do attack?' she asked.

He grinned, yet again. 'Under the cart.'

'I'll remember that.'

'Actually we're puzzled why they haven't bothered us more from the air. Especially as they captured our heavy anti-aircraft battery while the buggers were half-asleep.'

'Don't you have *anything* that can hit back?' she said.

'There's a good Sikh ack ack unit. They're OK.' He gave her one of his direct looks. 'Are you interested in that sort of thing?'

'I am a military wife,' she reminded him. 'One of those plucky little women. And my father was big in the army.' She shifted round to address him face to face. 'You said it might come to a fight here. If it does, what troops have we got to put up against them?'

'Are you sure you want to know?'

'Try me.'

'Well there's us, of course – the KOYLIS. Don't s'pose the name means much to you.'

'Hold on...KOYLIS...I used to know this. King's Own Light Infantry. Is that Yorkshire?'

'West Yorkshire. I'm impressed.'

'Don't be. What else?'

'Oh we're a rag-tag bunch. A lot of these blokes went through the Sittang River business – swam across, mostly. That's why we look such a shambles. Let's see. There's the Cameronians. The Burma Rifles – those that haven't already deserted. The 1st Royal Inskilling Fusiliers, to give them their full title. They only joined at Magwe – poor devils don't know what's hit them. Um...we've got Punjabis, Rajputs and Sikhs. Gurkhas, thank god. Some good local men – Kachins, Chins...'

'Didn't I see a tank further back?' Jean said.

'Yes of course, 7th Hussars and 2nd Royal Tanks. What else? Oh I don't know. Is that enough for you?'

'I'll say.'

He lowered his voice. 'It's not as good as it sounds, Jean. These men have been through a lot. It's only sheer bloody-mindedness keeps 'em going.'

Soon after that the bullock cart stopped in its tracks as the whole twisting line of transports was brought to a halt. All down the line drivers switched off their engines and animals stood in the sun. Soldiers cursed with a vivid display of imagery. Before long Bruce got a radio message detailing the situation. He relayed it to the men and – in the late afternoon – expanded the explanation for Jean's benefit.

'You know about *chaungs*?' he said.

'*Chaungs*? You mean those little tributaries off a river?'

'Yeah. This is a tale of two *chaungs*. We crossed one a mile or so back. Now the Japs have taken it over, so that cuts off any avenue of retreat. Then there's another *chaung* a couple of miles ahead – called Pin Chaung, apparently. And there's a ford over it – but guess what?'

'The Japanese are there too?'

'That's right. The little buggers have outflanked us. As usual. Outflanking is their favourite thing to do in the whole world. They're in a village called Twingon that overlooks the ford and they've got three field guns up there blocking the way.'

'So we're trapped?'

'We are,' he said grimly. River on the left. High ground on the right. *Chaungs* before and behind, both in Jap hands. They'll attack tomorrow. Look, if you three ladies want to leave us, you go ahead. You could try walking through the Jap positions. They *ought* to let refugees through.'

'I don't fancy that,' she told him. We'll stick with you, if we may.'

'Good. Very glad to have you. The problem is water. We're desperate for it and they've got the river covered. There's a kind've box canyon leading onto the Irrawaddy further back. A water cart's been down there but the position's very exposed.'

She thought for a moment. 'You know, there's a sort of mansion overlooking the river half a mile on.' She pointed ahead. 'They've got a pool. I know, 'cos I've swum in it.'

His head jerked up. 'Is there now? I'd better tell Scott about that.'

'Scott?'

'Our commanding officer. A good man.' He got onto the radio and spoke briefly to an intelligence officer.

'What about attacking the Japanese at this village?' she asked, after he'd finished. 'Is that possible?'

'At Twingon? Funny you should mention that, because the Chinese have sent a regiment down here to help us out. And they *have* been detailed to attack Twingon.'

The men were listening in to their conversation and an old hand called Simpson, whose girth resembled Sergeant Johnson's, broke out '*Oh no, sir*! Not them! Not the sodding Chinks!'

Jean was familiar with soldiery's colourful vocabulary from her time with the Glosters, but being at war clearly took things up a level. Mention of the Chinese unlocked a volley of obscenities that trumped anything she'd heard before.

'Not them Chinese!' exclaimed the man whose arm was in plaster. 'Fuck me to buggery.'

'Fuck me too,' said a lugubrious character called Stebbings. 'And fuck my Auntie Rose while you're about it.'

'Now men,' Bruce reproved them. 'There are ladies present.'

'No, no,' Jean protested. The last thing she wanted was the men feeling constrained by their presence. It was a pity Jyoti had to hear it, but the girl would be exposed to much more than swearing. 'Swear away, lads,' she told them. 'We're used to it. In fact my husband's the one soldier I know who doesn't swear. Anyway, what's wrong with the Chinese?'

'What's wrong with 'em?' cried Simpson passionately. 'What's wrong with 'em?'

His rhetorical enquiry brought a low growling sound from the men that swelled to an unnerving volume. The woodwork trembled under its impulse.

'What's wrong wiv 'em?' Simpson repeated again. 'Tell me, sir – 'ave the little yeller buggers actually attacked Twingon then?'

'Well, not as yet,' answered Bruce.

'No, not as yet, sir,' said Simpson.

'Not as bollocking yet,' cried an inoffensive little chap in the corner.

'No, nor they won't neither,' Stebbings cried. 'We'd wait for ever afore they did. We could go to the end of the sodding road, to the hellest of hells where Judas lost 'is bollocking boots, before *they* attack.'

'What it is, ma'am,' explained arm-in-plaster with surprising patience, 'Is them Chinks, they ain't got no sense of time, ma'am. So say you was to tell 'em – attack at lunchtime – well then at lunchtime the bollocking little buggers'd still be eatin' their breakfast – whatever they 'ave for breakfast, an' I 'ate to think about that.'

Stebbings reinforced the point. 'Yes ma'am, an' if you tell 'em – attack at dinner time – then at dinner time they'd still be doin' their ablutions, ma'am, an' polishin' their little yeller arses.'

'I'm sorry I started this,' Jean said.

'In any case, ain't no point them attackin' Twingon,' Simpson said, 'Cos the perishin' little yeller devils ain't got no artillery and tanks 'ave they, the useless little bastards.'

'Now there you're wrong, Simpson,' Bruce pointed out, 'Because General Slim has just placed his guns and tanks under the command of this Chinese regiment. I have it on good authority.'

This latest news was absolutely shattering to the men – the last straw in a world that now passed all comprehension. Another sound issued from the cart, an unfathomable one until Jean realised it was a dozen men all spluttering at the same time.

'Then General Slim, bugger 'im – beggin' your pardon, sir – 'e ain't never gonna see 'is tanks again,' roared Simpson, 'Cos them thievin' little bastards'll 'ave 'em back in Chink-land soon as look at 'im. I don't believe this is 'appening, sir. No, I do not believe it.'

The outrage over Slim putting British tanks under Chinese command rumbled on for several hours. Stuck in the stranded cart, the men had nothing to do but grumble, and they made the most of it. Every now and then the sounds of lament subsided, then broke out again in another form. Only when the light began to fail and the prospect of an evening meal loomed was their attention diverted elsewhere.

Jean had discussed this meal with Deepa, and she now broached the subject with Bruce.

'Do you have a decent-sized stove in the cart?'

'We've got a stove and we've got pans. What we haven't got is someone who can cook a decent meal. Simpson did the last one and three men went off sick.'

'Ah but you do have someone,' she told him. 'Deepa's a wonderful cook. And I can help her. Do you mind if we have a go?'

'Are you kidding? Please, be our guest.'

They selected from the store of tins in the cart and added some of their own rice. Deepa found some herbs from her bag. She even climbed from the cart and darted towards an unpromising shrub at the roadside, returning with a handful of dusty leaves. Best of all she was able to add water to the concoction in the pan, because water carts were now coming down the line of stationary vehicles to ragged, croaking cheers from the men. It seemed that Jean's tip about the swimming pool had paid off.

As night came down the whole area of sandy ridges was dotted with small fires, where men boiled billy cans to make the most essential element in the soldier's life: tea. This activity made the landscape look more palatable than it did in daylight.

While Deepa and Jean worked at the stove and the men sniffed the unfamiliar aroma of home cooking, Bruce talked to Jyoti. She'd taken Bear from her bag and was holding him in her arms.

'Who's that?' Bruce asked.

'It's Bear.'

'I can see it's a bear, but what's his name?'

'No, his name *is* Bear. Well, I don't know his real name because I found him – so I just call him "Bear".'

'That doesn't seem right, Jyoti. I mean, suppose I just called you "Girl". What would you think?'

She thought about this. 'I wouldn't like it very much.'

'Exactly. But anyway it's obvious this bear already has a name. He's Herbert.'

'Herbert!' Jyoti inspected Bear at arms' length. 'Do you think so?'

'There's no doubt about it. Look at those Herberty legs. And you can see it in his eyes. Look, try calling him Herbert to his face.'

'Um...I don't know.'

'Give it a try.'

'All right.' She held the bear close and addressed it shyly. 'Hello Herbert.'

'There. Did you see the reaction in his eyes?'

'I'm not sure.'

'Oh Jyoti, come on. Believe me, he's Herbert. If he's not Herbert, then I'm a Dutchman.'

'All right then, I'll try again. Hello Herbert.' She nodded. 'Yes, it sounds right now. Thank you, Mr...'

'No, not "Mr", please. That would be like calling me "Man". I'm Bruce.'

'Thank you, Bruce.'

'It's a pleasure, Jyoti.'

Jean overheard the exchange and was struck by the way Jyoti had been drawn out of herself since their first tight-lipped meeting in Rangoon a mere matter of weeks earlier. There was an irony to it, given what the girl had already endured on the road, and would doubtless endure in future. Jean was grateful to Bruce for taking trouble with her. Of course there was irony in this too – a young officer discussing a teddy bear with an 11-year old, when the next day he might kill or be killed on the battlefield.

Deepa and Jean were left in no doubt about the meal's success. The men disposed of it voraciously and had there been second and third helpings – which there weren't – they'd have vanished as rapidly as the first. Fulsome tributes came their way, the imperfections of Chinese troops clean forgotten. They even had men from other units drifting past the cart, drawn by the aroma – and quickly sent on their way with another bout of profanity.

Later that evening Bruce thanked her personally. The cooking fires had been extinguished one by one as a red night sky settled over the unlovely hills of Yenangyaung. The men fell asleep early, scattered around the cart coughing and wheezing and farting, and calling out plaintively to their wives or mothers. Jyoti slept with her head on Deepa's breast. Jean and Bruce were still awake, leaning against the side-board of the cart.

'Thank you for that meal,' Bruce said quietly. 'Please let Deepa know how much it was appreciated. You know it's true – that old saw about an army marching on its stomach. My lot haven't been this animated for weeks. In fact having you three on board has been a great success.'

'For us,' she said.

She could see his features clearly under moonlight and his eyes upon her. She liked the openness about his face and the way he was always grinning. His knees, in their khaki shorts, were close to hers. They'd only talked about food but there was intimacy in the air and both of them were aware of it.

'You know it could be rough tomorrow,' he said.

'It's all right. We do know.'

'I don't know what to suggest for you three. No-one can predict where a shell will fall.'

'Especially if it's fired by the Chinese.'

He laughed out loud, prompting Simpson to lurch upright, still asleep, and then subside again.

'It would be awful to see your little girl get hurt,' Bruce said.

'Look, don't worry about us. You've got your job to do. We'll try to help if anyone gets wounded.' She sought words that would put his mind at rest. 'Deepa knows the risks. Jyoti's already come close to death since we left Rangoon.'

'So you've come all that way,' he said. 'It must have been an awful upheaval for you when the bombs began to fall.'

She squirmed at the thought of her former life. 'This will sound strange, Bruce, because those were horrible events, but actually for me it was good. I was ridiculous in Rangoon. We'd lived in Burma several years and I knew nothing. I lived the expatriate life, and you know what that's like – well, you probably don't, but I promise you it's nothing.' She felt all the bitterness about herself spilling out, to a man she hardly knew. 'I was as shallow as the worst of them. I was *silly*. In all my time there I learnt nothing – nothing that was important. I used to think Burmans were nice because they smiled at me in the markets. When the troubles started I was amazed at the way they persecuted the Indians. I knew nothing. There are no excuses.'

'I think you're great,' he said.

She gave a little sigh, half way to a sob. 'I'm not great, Bruce.'

They were both quiet for a while. It seemed natural to sit beside him not saying anything. The only sounds came from the cicadas, punctuated by the ludicrous screaming of mules.

'I can kind've sympathise with the Burmese,' he said eventually. 'Oh I know they're unreliable. There's a lot of them out here helping the Japs. Even the ones we've got in the Burma Rifles – they're slipping off home when they get the chance. At the same time, if you think about it they don't owe us anything. We treat them like dirt – the way we treat everyone who isn't British, though what's so great about us I wonder.'

Jean was glad of the darkness because she could feel her face growing red. He mightn't know it, but she was one of the people he alluded to.

After a bit his voice came again. 'Let's face it, the Brits come out here to make money. As far as I can see we've done little for the Burmese. All right, we've taken oil from the ground, but only for our own benefit. And anyway we'll be blowing all that to smithereens.' He looked up at the oil derricks, visible on the sky-line. 'I'm surprised it hasn't happened already.'

Behind him one of the men turned over, muttering gibberish.

'Even the paddle-steamers,' Bruce went on, 'I suppose you could say they *have* been a contribution, opening up communications and so on. Now they're being scuttled up and down the Irrawaddy so the Japs can't get their hands on 'em. It's almost a symbol of what we've done here. Between us, we and the Japs are destroying a whole way of life.'

This is so right, she thought, so absolutely right. It's odd but it must be the situation we're in that makes me seem close to a complete stranger; the intimacy of the wooden cart, the night, the imminence of danger in the morning. She'd have liked him to reach out and put a hand on hers, but knew he wouldn't. She wondered how the two of them could have turned out so differently. He was army, like her, yet here he was with thoughts that she recognised as obvious only now he'd put them into words.

'I managed to catch glimpses of the real Burma,' he said. 'Small towns we passed through. The young women out in the streets in their colourful clothes, flowers in their hair, jewellery and little velvet slippers, gay parasols. No suffragette movement there. They had what they wanted. Well not now. Not any more.'

'Do you like women, Bruce?' she asked.

He turned his direct look onto her. 'Yes, I do.'

When Jean lay down beside Deepa to sleep, the Indian opened her eyes and smiled conspiratorially.

'Nice, madam,' she whispered.

'Stop it,' Jean whispered back. 'I'm a married woman.'

Next morning the atmosphere felt very different. Jean remembered a

Hemingway novel that distinguished between night and morning moods in battle – the latter more sombre – and she recognised the force of those sentiments now. Their situation was so precarious and the Yenangyaung landscape so dispiriting. The men too were silent and preoccupied. As they slurped the inevitable morning mugs of tea a distraction occurred, to put it mildly. From the direction of town came a series of massive explosions, far greater than anything the Japanese could have put together. A fog of black smoke rose hundreds of metres high from beyond the ridges, and through the smoke, great tongues of flame. Jean had never seen such an awesome spectacle, and to judge by their reaction the men hadn't either.

'So they've done it,' Bruce observed. 'Crude oil, millions of gallons going up in smoke. That'll get the Japs going. They needed it as much as we did.'

Another series of explosions followed, like outsize fire-crackers on Guy Fawkes night.

'What is it now, sir?' asked Stebbings.

'Individual buildings going up in smoke,' Bruce told him. 'The power-house will be last. When that goes nothing in Yenangyaung will work any more.' He gazed at the horizon. 'Well, the Japs are welcome to the place.'

In what was to be the last peaceful moment of the day Jean watched Bruce approach a podgy American war correspondent who'd made his camp under a banyan tree. Several British soldiers did the same, all of them handing over letters. She wondered who Bruce's letter was addressed to. Then all hell broke loose.

For one reason and another, her memories of that long day were highly selective. Maybe because for much of the time she was face down in the cart, or under the cart. Maybe because that much frenzied, thunderous action couldn't *be* absorbed and retained in the usual way. Or maybe her brain had just eliminated scenes she found too distressing. Even so, she remembered Japanese planes bombing the column, transports scattering in all directions, mules bolting noisily across the ridges, a British soldier in flames running in crazy circles. She came to identify the curious 'crump' sound as the Japanese fired mortars across their position, the closest shave being one that left a crater 20 yards from where they sat. She saw the enemy's machine gunners emerging from their positions ('Out in the open at last,' cried a British officer) and British infantry crawling up ridges towards them with fixed bayonets. There were things she didn't understand at all till they were explained to her afterwards, like the tank commander riskily sticking his head out of the turret so that he could radio Japanese mortar positions to British artillery. And there were things made memorable because they were so quaint and unusual, as when British soldiers cut open the water pipes that criss-crossed the ridges outside Yenangyaung, and with the inferno raging, clustered around with canteens and water bottles like wasps at a honey pot.

Towards the end of the day Bruce's unit attacked Japanese troops stationed by a water tank on the high hills above the oilfields. Later they dynamited the tank and found a few inches of rusty water at the bottom. That night they made camp up against the tank's steel walls and for once felt safe from ground attack. Jean dressed the minor wounds of two men – the unit had got off lightly – while Deepa prepared another evening meal. Jyoti chattered blithely to the men, apparently unaffected by what she'd witnessed. She'd been adopted by them as a sort of mascot.

As she lay down to sleep that night Jean reflected that – in spite of everything – she was glad to have been where she was and to have seen what she saw. She'd come from a military family and married a soldier, but until that day had no real conception of what it was to be in a battle. Now she knew – something, at least – of the pain and misery the men endured and the courage they showed. She wondered whether the experience would have made her a better wife to Philip.

Morning saw no alleviation of their situation. Water remained an acute problem, especially for the animals. The heat was like nothing she had ever encountered and with the heat came flies, in black clouds. The men were sitting ducks for bombers and for machine guns from the fighters. A new hazard came from the oil derricks. Smoke still billowed from that direction but Japanese snipers had managed to climb high onto the metal structures, whence they could fire down upon the British.

When the bullock cart changed its position, the legacy of the previous day's fighting was quickly apparent. At the roadside, the bloated bodies of friend and foe alike lay in heaps, blackened in the heat. Even Jyoti recoiled from their stench.

To Jean, who had now observed a single day's fighting, it seemed impossible for men to do this day after day. But that was what Scott's forces had done, first at Sittang, then Magwe, then marching north to Yenangyaung to do it all over again. Small wonder the men resembled punch-drunk fighters at the bell for the 12th round. And the previous day's fighting had got them nowhere because the entire force was still trapped near the river, encircled by the Japanese. Jean could sense the claustrophobia of men stuck in a trap. It was hard to see how the affair could end. They would die here from thirst and dehydration if shells and bullets eluded them. Yet surrendering to Japanese forces was not something to be contemplated lightly with the outcome so dependent on the whims of individual commanders. Word quickly got round about atrocities. The previous day the Japanese had captured 300 British troops, roped them in batches of eight and marched them south, bayoneting stragglers.

By mid-day, after a morning under heavy fire, the British troops were close to desperation. It was at this point that Bruce received a radio message from one of Scott's officers. The men in the cart listened anxiously to the one-sided conversation.

'OK sir, we'll give it a try,' he finished up. 'Hassan,' he called to the Indian driving the cart, 'We're making a dash for it. Follow that tank up ahead. Wherever it goes, you go.'

'Yes sir, right sir,' the Indian cried.

The men cheered as they lurched into motion, seeing some activity as better than none.

'What's happening, sir?' called Simpson, who had long ago appointed himself the official link between Bruce and the men.

'Seems like 2nd Royal Tanks have found something,' Bruce told them. 'They were out hunting Japs and found a track that leads to the *chaung* – or so they say. Very narrow – just room for a tank, apparently. It comes out about a mile downstream from the ford.'

'Yes sir, but can we get across?' enquired Simpson.

'That's what we're going to find out.' Bruce's expression was unusually grim. 'I doubt whether all our vehicles will go, but it's worth a try.'

The men cheered again as their cart wheeled round to join the exodus. After the enforced inactivity Jean too felt excitement rising within her. Everything was happening at once. Vehicles of every description jockeyed for position. Soldiers shouted madly, mules brayed and muleteers prodded their recalcitrant animals which ran in all directions or dug in their heels. Three Japanese fighters swooped down spraying machine gun fire and a Sikh ack ack unit responded, bringing one aircraft down trailing black smoke amidst a crescendo of cheering. Jyoti stood up in the cart yelling her head off and Deepa, furious, pulled her straight down again. Jean sympathised with the girl; it was hard not to get caught up in the moment.

Naturally there was plenty of speculation as to whether the men of Royal Tanks were capable of identifying a useful track – or anything at all – but doubts began to fall away as the bullock-cart joined a bottleneck of vehicles manoeuvring into single file at the narrow point of access.

'We're heading north, at least,' Bruce muttered. 'If this goes far enough it'll have to lead to the *chaung*.'

After half a mile they hit the problem Bruce had predicted, when the track's firm surface gave way to sand. Some vehicles got horribly stuck and had to be manhandled to the side, including several ambulances. Some of the wounded were taken out and transferred to the tanks, positioned along the sides like sardines in a can. Those in the worst condition had to be left behind, a horrible decision for any commander to take. As Bruce had also foretold, the bullocks negotiated sand in the same manner – no better, no worse – that they tackled any other surface.

The mules too were at home on this ground, but in other respects these creatures, half-crazed with thirst, presented an utterly woebegone appearance. Jean expected that at any minute they would lie down beside the track and refuse to move. And then in a single moment everything changed. A gaggle of mules ahead of them pricked up their ears and began braying furiously. They quickened their pace and were soon charging along, leaving muleteers hopelessly in their wake.

'What's going on?' exclaimed arm-in-plaster.

Bruce was on his feet, almost dancing with agitation. 'It's got to be water! They've scented water.'

Now the bullocks reacted too, accelerating from their habitual trudge to a pace approaching a canter, something no-one had seen before. The cart rocked wildly as the Indian driver abused his charges, now beyond his control. For that matter nobody was in control. The cart was one element in a headlong charge for the *chaung*.

The moment that they hit the *chaung* was an epiphany. They emerged from the dismal landscape that had held them for so long onto a broad, sandy creek, with the sunlight bouncing off two feet of water. The Japanese, who'd been noticeably absent from the track, now reappeared on a ridge to their left, spraying the area with machine gun fire. Unaware of the danger, mules congregated in the shallows to drink. Some soldiers followed their example, discipline abandoned, throwing themselves at the water's edge heedless of the bullets kicking up sand all around them. Vehicles fanned out to take the crossing and the peaceful stretch of water became a maelstrom of grinding engines and churned-up sand. Most vehicles that had got this far managed to make it. The tanks went across with consummate ease. A couple of lorries had to be abandoned mid-stream.

The cart's problem was that the bullocks wanted to stop for water too. The Indian driver flailed away with his whip and two of the men, showing presence of mind, jumped overboard with buckets, presenting water to the animals on the hoof. Still the danger wasn't over. Japanese positions on the ridge allowed fire to be directed down at a steep angle, and bullets began to rake the cart. A soldier went down clutching his neck, then the driver yelped and fell backwards onto the men. Simpson was on his feet with surprising speed, grabbing the whip to flay the bullocks and unleashing a stream of profanity such as the creatures had never known. Jean fancied that one of them raised its head in astonishment.

Another soldier went down and Bruce shouted above the pandemonium, urging the three females to get over the side. He stood and physically lifted them one by one into the water, so that the cart was between them and the direction of fire.

'Stay alongside and keep your heads down,' he bellowed.

In this manner they reached the far side of the *chaung* and scrambled up a rise into an unexpected belt of trees. Deepa led, dragging Jyoti behind her. As Jean followed, a man stepped from the security of the copse to pull her to safety. He was a scruffy-looking individual wearing a buccaneering hat, but something about his demeanour inspired calm when all around was chaos.

'Thanks a lot,' she told him.

'It's a pleasure,' he said. 'Nice to meet an English lady out for a stroll.'

Only as she moved away did Jean realise that her helper had a general's insignia on his shoulder. An infantryman standing nearby said 'Do you realise who that was, miss?'

'No, who was it?'

'That's Slim, innit. The big cheese.'

'I'm sorry?'

'General Slim, miss. 'E's the bloke wot's in charge.'

Once they got going bullocks were hard to stop and the cart had rumbled on for a further 20 yards. Catching up with it, she found Simpson lying full length and a couple of grim-faced men around him. Blood dribbled from his mouth and there was more of it on his shirt front.

He grimaced on seeing her. ''Ello miss. Bleedin' Japs, eh? Bollockin' little buggers.'

She reached for the buttons of his shirt. 'Let me have a look at that.'

He shook his head. 'It's all right, miss. You can't do nothin'. Go an' 'ave a look at your young man.'

'My young...!'

He nodded towards the far end of the cart. 'Over there. Now you look after 'im, eh.'

She squeezed Simpson's hand and crossed to where Bruce lay face down on the boards.

'We didn't want to move 'im, miss,' said Stebbings.

A bullet had passed through his left shoulder blade. She knew it had happened when he was standing in the cart, heaving her over the side.

## ~ Eight ~

## North on the Chindwin

The hours after the Pin Chaung crossing were a period of retrenchment for Scott's forces, as the wounded were attended to and the dead bodies dealt with. Men who'd been displaced from stranded vehicles were reallocated to other transport. It seemed Scott was in no hurry to move his forces on, and against a background of noise and confusion each unit did its best with casualties. As the only person in the bullock cart with medical experience Jean felt responsibility weigh heavily upon her. There had been five casualties and she made a quick check of each. The Indian driver was dead. The man shot in the neck was still breathing but she held out no hope of survival. The same was true of Simpson, who'd given an accurate 'old soldier's' diagnosis of his own downfall. Another man had taken a bullet in the leg. And there was Bruce.

Her instinct was to give Bruce priority but she had to be fair to the others. She considered this. The two men mortally wounded needed morphine, if she could get it, and the leg wound could wait. So she did have licence to attend to Bruce, and the men crowded round urging her to do just that – a measure of his popularity. Heart in mouth, she cut away his shirt to check the damage. A bullet had gone through the right shoulder. She got the men gently to turn him over and gave a little gasp of hope on seeing the bullet wound's exit mark near the nipple.

'Will 'e be all right, miss?' Stebbings was hovering anxiously.

'I don't know,' she told him. 'There's a chance, but I'm going to need equipment we haven't got.'

'Excuse me, miss,' said the frail little chap whose nickname was 'Tiger', 'But there's a medical lorry a hundred yards away. Can I get something for you?'

'That's wonderful,' she said. 'Look, I'll go because I know what I want.

But thanks for the information.'

Deepa was at her elbow. 'Helping, madam?'

There was nobody she would rather have helping her. 'Yes please, Deepa. We're going to need boiling water, so everything can be sterilised.'

'Yes madam.'

She took another look at Bruce and thought hard. This was where two months training from Matron in the Rangoon hospital ought to kick in, if only she could get it right. Bruce, mumbling but still unconscious, was breathing in a laboured fashion. Jean took his pulse, which was high. She reckoned these were signs of a condition – the medical term eluded her – where blood collected in the space between the chest wall and the lung. Since the bullet had passed right through Bruce's body she judged – or did that mean hoped? – that it had missed the scapula and the rib cage, and with any luck the vital organs too. If there was such a thing as a 'good' trunk wound, this might be it. Jean actually caught herself crossing fingers, which was as unprofessional as a nurse could get. Matron would have hauled her over the coals had she seen it.

The trouble was she needed to draw off that blood, or there was every risk the lung would collapse. And it had to be done in a hurry.

'I need an aspirator,' she announced, to no-one in particular.

The men stared at her blankly.

She climbed out of the cart. 'I'm going to try the medical lorry. If I find what I'm looking for we'll need power – electrical, battery, I don't care.'

'I'll look after that, miss,' said Stebbings. There's a truck full of

Sappers over there. They can handle anything. You go and get your aspidistra.'

She ran like a mad woman until the red cross of the medical lorry appeared in her vision. A single nurse was inside, a girl about Jean's age. She was willing, but bewildered.

Jean explained the situation and was told there were no doctors available; one had been killed and the other had his hands full with emergencies.

'I'll need some morphine,' Jean said, breathing heavily from her 100-yard dash. 'And I need an aspirator.'

The girl looked blank. 'What's that when it's at home?'

Jean had a rummage herself, in the large multi-drawered cabinet where the equipment was stowed. After a bit she found what she wanted.

'I'll bring it back,' she told the girl. 'Meanwhile I'll be working in a bullock cart just this side of the *chaung*.'

'What's a *chaung*?' the girl said.

Jean explained.

'Here's the morphine,' the nurse said. 'Sorry I wasn't much help.'

'You were fine.'

Back in the cart, she gave morphine to the two dying men. Deepa had somehow secured a clean towel and spread it on the wooden boards. It was the best that could be done against the acute danger of infection. A Sapper stood by and Jean showed him the aspirator.

'I need to get some power for this,' she told him. 'I don't know how.'

'You leave that to me love,' he told her.

After putting her pitiful supply of equipment – rubber gloves included

— into Deepa's pan of boiling water, she cleaned and patched the wound in Bruce's back, then got the men to lay him gently on the towel. By some sleight-of-hand the Sapper had got the aspirator pumping. With her heart banging furiously in her breast she inserted the needle into the chest wound and watched the bloody fluid being drawn off into the glass jar. Behind her the groans of the wounded subsided as the morphine did its job. The other men gathered round her, all eyes on the medical procedure. One of them quietly passed out against the side of the cart.

When she judged that the device had done its work she removed the needle and bandaged the wound. Had she possessed any sort of religious faith she'd have prayed. As it was she could only wait, and hope. There was still no sign of the unit being mobilised, so Bruce was spared the lurching of a moving cart. And Simpson and the other man were able to die in peace. The hiatus in troop movements was explained late in the afternoon. Chinese outfits had at last attacked the Japanese at Twingon, and routed them. It was better than nothing, but their tardiness had led to many unnecessary deaths. Even so Bruce's men received the news almost placidly. Without Simpson, their cheer-leader, swearing seemed to have lost its savour. Profanity did make a brief reprise when more bad news reached them late at night. A young gunner officer had taken a truck back across the *chaung* to retrieve the wounded who'd been left behind, but found them all dead, bayoneted or with their throats cut.

Jean's visit to the medical lorry had consequences. In the middle of dinner that evening she received a visit from the doctor. He apologised for interrupting her meal but went ahead anyway with a stream of questions designed to suss out her medical competence. At the end of it he asked if she'd be willing to help with casualties from other units. Some of Bruce's men objected to this – 'She's ours,' Stebbings cried – but Jean could hardly say 'no'. In fact she wanted to help.

The doctor stared at the men tucking into Deepa's evening meal and sniffed the aroma of cooking appreciatively. 'You men seem to have got yourself set up very nicely,' he observed.

The moment Jean laid her head down that night she was out for the count. The men let her sleep on, and she woke as they were eating breakfast. Stebbings immediately shoved a mug of tea into her hands.

'You deserve this, miss. Now what do you want to eat?'

'The same as you,' she told him.

'We've got some good news,' said Stebbings.

'What do you mean?'

He indicated with a nod of his head, and she turned to see Bruce half-sitting up, biting into an army biscuit. He looked pale but cheerful.

'What the hell are you doing?' she said.

'I'm hungry.'

'You have a life-threatening injury. You can't go racketing around whenever you feel like it.'

He grinned. 'Sorry Matron.'

The men laughed and eventually she did too. In that severe response, masking her emotion, there'd been more than an echo of her old boss in Rangoon.

'Well how do you feel?' she asked him.

'I feel OK. You have to be to tackle one of these biscuits.'

'Then please finish eating it. I'm going to examine you.'

She checked his wounds and changed the dressings. The results pleased and intrigued her. He seemed to have rallied with almost absurd speed. She'd seen something similar in the Rangoon hospital, but was still astonished by it.

'It was worth getting shot,' he murmured, 'To have you minister to me.'

'Don't be ridiculous,' she said, to conceal how much she liked him saying it. 'You're to stay lying down for the next 24 hours, and don't you forget it.'

'The men say you saved my life.'

'And what do they know. I'm fully aware of how you got yourself injured. It was a reckless thing to do.'

'Yes matron.'

All around her the men were grinning.

Scott's troops did get moving again shortly afterwards. Slim had withdrawn them to the region of Mount Popa, 40 miles north of Yenangyaung, recognising that for the time being these men had had enough. They were also woefully short of equipment. In crossing Pin Chaung, Scott had left behind his howitzers and 25-pounders, and a couple of Bofors guns.

After Yenangyaung, their new site seemed ridiculously peaceful. It was greener, and the imposing bulk of Mount Popa loomed above them. The troops were given time to lick their wounds, the military equivalent of R&R. In fact the medics were amongst the busiest people around. Jean was used as an auxiliary nurse/doctor much as she had been in Rangoon, albeit in less comfortable circumstances. She was on her feet ten hours a day. When it was dark she fell asleep early, tired out. Despite – or because of – the hours of hard labour she felt tremendously well.

She was also as happy as she could ever remember, and not only because the work was so worthwhile. Every evening before sleeping she spent time talking with a recuperating Bruce, and the thought of it sustained her during the day. She loved the way she felt in his company but it also worried her. She was a married woman, and whatever the problems with Philip she'd never remotely considered straying with another man. It wasn't something decent women did. She wasn't 'considering' it now but things happened beyond her control. She was too gauche to surmise what *he* felt. He obviously enjoyed her company and was friendly and considerate and – a new experience – interested in what she said, but he never behaved in any way improperly. Sometimes, during the moments before she drifted off to sleep, she wished he would.

While Jean worked, Deepa and Jyoti also flourished in their new surroundings. The men were unused to the company of women and made the most of it. They found all sorts of spurious reasons to consult Deepa, especially about food. The fame of her cooking spread well beyond the bullock cart. She prepared meals for some 30 men, to their satisfaction and the envy of the rest. But popular as she was, she couldn't compete with Jyoti. The girl had changed utterly from the introspective creature of the Rangoon days. Always lively and communicative, ever curious, she quickly found her way into the affections of men stranded from their families in a distant land. She chattered away to all-comers and was adopted by the whole division. Herbert, introduced to everyone she met, became a kind of divisional mascot.

When they'd been at Mount Popa for a week, Jean was summoned to meet Major-General Scott, the divisional commander. The men were suitably impressed.

'Gawd miss, you'll 'ave to watch yer P's and Q's,' Stebbings told her.

'You're for the high jump now,' said Bruce. 'What have you been up to?'

'Sabotage?' said Jean. 'It could've been that.'

Scott was in a tent containing a make-shift table and several chairs. He stood as she entered and shook her hand warmly.

'Mrs Costain?'

She nodded. 'Jean.'

'Bruce Scott.'

Another Bruce, she thought; they're everywhere. She reckoned this one was about 50. A good-looking bloke, in spite of the stresses and strains that were visible on his face. He managed to appear alert and relaxed at the same time. They both sat as he continued.

'I've heard about your activities, Jean, and I want to thank you on behalf of all the men.'

'Thank you, sir.'

'I've been trying to get some information about your husband, without success I'm afraid.'

'The last time I saw him was in Yenangyaung.'

'Yes, of course. Look, I have a proposition for you. It's beginning to look as if this division will stay around here, for a few more weeks anyway. That being so, I'm concerned about the wounded men. I'm having them moved out in lorries.'

'Where would they go?' she asked, wondering why he was telling her this.

'We have a couple of hospital ships on the Chindwin – the *Thumingala* and the *Mysore*. So far they've been respected by the Japs.' He crossed his fingers. 'Hope it stays that way – you can't trust the buggers. There's a ferry at a place called Sameikka, where the Irrawaddy branches east towards Mandalay. Our lorries will cross there and pick up one of the hospital ships.'

'That sounds good.'

'Yes, but the journey takes a couple of days and these men will need constant care. What I'm inviting you to do is to accompany them up to the handover and deal with all their medical needs.'

Jean was nonplussed. 'Me! Would there be a doctor as well?'

'No, there wouldn't.'

'Blimey. I'm not sure I could...'

He interrupted her. 'We know what you can do, Jean. My spies are everywhere.'

She laughed. 'There's just one problem...'

For the second time he butted in. 'Your Indian friend and her daughter? Again, the three of you are quite famous round here. I gather you're known as 'The holy trinity' in some quarters. And like the holy trinity, you're indivisible. It's all right – all three of you would go. Actually I have some misgivings on that score, because you ladies have been good for the division's morale. But needs must.'

Jean didn't cavil again. 'In that case, if you're sure it's OK...'

'You'll do it?'

'Yes.'

'Thank you. Thank you very much. I ought to have said, the transfer will be made at Monywa. They won't allow you onto the hospital ship, but you should pick up a paddle steamer easily enough to take the three of you north to Kalewa.'

He stood, Jean along with him, and they shook hands again. 'And thanks, Jean, for all you've done. It won't be forgotten.'

She went back and gave the news to Deepa and Jyoti. All three thought themselves fortunate to be given this leg-up on the next stage of their journey. At the same time they were surprised to find that leaving the division would be a wrench. In a short time they'd become part of something that was important to them. And Jean had gained an insight into the regimental loyalties that flourished in the British army.

The news of their imminent departure got around, and in the 48 hours before they left an extraordinary number of men passed by the bullock cart to say goodbye, in many cases passing on small gifts of food. They were overwhelmed by the attention. When the cavalcade of wounded men finally pulled out in three lorries, a big crowd gathered to wave them off. Much of the attention focussed on the three females, who stood at the tailgate waving back, and in Jyoti's case jumping up and down on the spot. There was also a surprise. The division's photographer had been busy, and a picture of Jyoti holding Herbert had been blown up to an imposing size and fastened to the front of three tanks from the 7th Hussars, who roared into line alongside the departing lorries. Jean felt sorry to be leaving all over again.

There was one reason she *wasn't* sorry, because Bruce was amongst the men being transported out. He'd argued against it, claiming he was perfectly fit to stay with the fighting men, but the medics were having none of it. Jean was relieved because his sort of injury needed a period of recuperation, but also because it gave her two more days in his company. In the event the congested lorries afforded no scope for the kind of conversation they'd come to enjoy. And in any case Jean was hard at work most of the time.

They crossed on the Sameikka ferry very early the following morning. Nothing else moved on the flat landscape. In a chill mist the broad sweep of the Irrawaddy had a bleak air that foreshadowed her sense of imminent parting. The Karen ferrymen, who were experts at this kind of work, sang dirge-like hymns that further depressed her spirits. Even Jyoti was subdued. As the army lorries left the scene the Karens were throwing grenades into the river to kill some fish for their dinner.

After the ferry they drove up the east bank of the Chindwin to Monywa. The hospital ship *Mysore* was waiting for them. The walking wounded boarded first, then orderlies carried the rest on with stretchers. Jean talked to the medical director and handed over some notes about the serious cases. The man advised her to get a passage up-river on the stern-wheeler *Siam*, which was moored further up the bank and due to leave the following morning.

Bruce had stood aside from the lively activity at the riverside, and Jean went across to him.

'Let's not say goodbye here,' he said. 'Come down the bank a bit.'

'I'll be five minutes,' she told Deepa, who was standing nearby with Jyoti.

They walked 100 yards until they were quite alone. Already the dusk was coming down with its usual tropical haste. The river was calm and the moored steamers jigged almost imperceptibly on its surface.

She put out a hand to clutch his arm. 'I really hate doing this.'

'Me too.'

'Bruce, I know it's been an awful time, but for me it's been the best time. I can't...' There were things she wanted to say but didn't feel free to do so. Most inconveniently, she started to imagine Philip looking on from a few yards away. 'I can't explain what I feel,' she ended lamely.

He gave her a page torn from a notebook. 'It looks as if our lot will end up in Calcutta. This is a forwarding address that will always find me. If anything comes up that you want to say, I want to hear it.'

A blast from the *Mysore's* funnel made her jump.

'That mean you have to go,' she said. 'Damn, damn, damn.'

He took the army rucksack off his shoulder and pulled something from it. 'This is a small stove that'll take wood as fuel. Where you're going you don't want to be carrying paraffin around.'

Her eyes filled up. 'How on earth did you manage that?'

Normally he'd have grinned, but not this time. 'I worked in a quartermaster's once. All the dodges.'

The funnel blasted again and they started towards it. The whole way back the words 'I love you' all but burst from her lips. Bruce shook hands with Deepa and Jyoti, gave her a quick smile, and went up the gang-plank without looking back.

Deepa murmured 'Nice, madam.'

Jean burst into floods of tears.

Next morning the *Siam* began its journey up-river. The Chindwin was the main tributary of the Irrawaddy, running roughly north-north-west for 400 miles. Kalewa, their destination, was the staging post marking the river's last navigable point north. *Siam's* passengers were mostly refugees, plus a handful of British soldiers, a few missionaries, and even some itinerant *hpoongyis* in their unmistakeable yellow robes. Jean reckoned there were six or seven hundred people on board and a crew member said the boat could take at least 300 more.

As usual the stern-wheeler's captain and most of the crew were Chittagonians. A Belgian missionary told Jean that manning these boats was becoming a problem. 'The Chittagonians are good men,' he explained, 'But they're...well, let's say they're not a very warlike race. Several steamers have been attacked from the air and that isn't their cup of tea, as you British say. Some of them slip away quietly. I can't say I blame them.'

'But the *Siam* seems to be well staffed,' Jean observed.

He agreed. 'Do not forget the British are scuttling boats all along this stretch of river – so that the Japanese can't get them, of course. A sad business, but it means there are still flotilla staff left over who want to work.'

While Deepa was taking a nap, Jean stood at the side-rail with Jyoti watching the world go by. Because of the humidity their clothes were already damp, but there was no question of feeling cold. In fact the motion of the boat gave some relief against the heat. Jean had never seen this part of Burma before and Jyoti, as always, was eager to take in every detail. After Yenangyaung the open landscape of bamboo and paddy fields had a liberating effect on her spirits. At the river's edge were stretches of very fine sand, almost white in colour. The *Siam* steamed past a number of well-populated villages and they saw the tops of pagodas behind trees, fishing boats in the water and chickens running about on shore. There was as much to see on the river itself, where all sorts of unseemly crafts – rafts, dugouts, Chinese junks – competed for the right of way, often hindering *Siam's* progress.

'Look!'

Jyoti pointed to the top of a funnel that was visible in the water ahead, a plangent apparition.

'What a sad sight,' Jean said. 'That was a proud paddle-steamer like this one not so long ago. Now it's been scuttled.'

'What's scuttled?' the girl asked. Her vocabulary had improved by leaps and bounds in the preceding weeks, and it was quite rare now to come across a word she didn't know.

'It's where someone sinks a boat on purpose,' Jean told her. One of Bruce's men had described how easy this process was, given the steamers' light steel hulls. 'They drill holes in the bottom,' she went on, 'Or they just fire a Sten gun through it.'

'It *is* sad,' Jyoti said.

She'd taken Herbert from her bag to show him the stricken vessel. Jean put a restraining arm on the girl's shoulder.

'Be *very* careful, Jyoti. If you drop Herbert overboard he'll be lost. He'd sink down to the river bed just like that steamer and stay there forever. We call it "a watery grave".'

'But couldn't we go back for him?' she said, nevertheless returning Herbert quickly to his bag.

'I'm afraid not. Look how quickly we're moving.'

This was unfortunate timing because as they both looked into the water a human corpse bobbed by. Its features were disfigured by a grotesque leer.

'Don't look,' said Jean quickly.

'It's all right.' Jyoti pointed again. 'There's another one!'

Jean knelt on the deck beside her. 'It doesn't bother you?'

'No, Jean. I know it's war. We've seen lots of things, haven't we?'

'Haven't we just.'

Jyoti giggled. '"Haven't we just!" What a funny way to say something.'

Jean smiled. They *had* seen a lot of things. In fact Jyoti had already witnessed more than most women would see in a lifetime. In all probability she'd see a lot more. Nothing could be done about it, but Jean wondered what damage was being inflicted on an 11-year old's mind. Already she felt tremendously protective of someone she'd only met a couple of months earlier. She kissed Jyoti and held her tight.

After a while they were joined at the handrail by the Belgian missionary. The man had made the journey many times before and was knowledgeable about customs of the river. He put Jean in mind of the Dutch tea-planter she'd met on their first paddle-steamer, not least in his excellent English.

Jyoti was intrigued by the two lascar seamen who stood in the bows, one each side, thrusting striped bamboo poles into the water and chanting in high, lachrymose voices.

'What *are* those men doing?' she said.

The Belgian laughed. 'Finding a way up this river is complicated. There are many things that can damage the boat or slow us down. Apart from those you can see – like that big log straight ahead – hundreds of sandbanks lie under the water, and the *Siam* can get stuck. The men with poles are finding out how deep the river is.'

'But why are they *singing*?' said Jyoti.

'It's their way of talking to the pilot, the man up on the poop – the most important person on the boat, by the way. He will know this bit of the river – maybe 50 miles of it – better than anyone. After him they will take on another pilot for the next 50 miles. So the men with the poles tell him about the river's depth, and he tells the helmsman where to go. Listen.'

He listened intently while one of the lascars chanted his weird utterances.

The Belgian translated. 'I think that was "Teen balm mila nahim", or something like that. It means he's put the pole all the way in and still not touched the bottom, so we're all right. The time to worry is when he sings very high. That means we're about to hit a sandbank.'

Without warning Jyoti opened her mouth and gave a grotesque imitation of the lascar's chant. 'Pole all the way, not touched bottom,' she sang. 'Pole all the way, not touched bottom.' This sparked a roar of laughter from other passengers on the deck.

Jean tapped her on the shoulder. 'Now then, Jyoti. Better not do that again, eh?'

The girl gave her cheeky grin. 'Sorry, Jean.' Now she pointed at the painted bamboo poles that stuck up six feet out of the water. 'And please sir, what are those poles for?'

'You don't have to answer all these questions,' Jean told the Belgian. 'She'll go on and on.'

'I really don't mind,' he said. 'Those are buoys.'

'Boys?' Jyoti frowned.

'Not like in boys and girls. Buoys – B-U-O-Y.'

'Another new word,' said Jean.

'They're to warn the pilot of dangers, like submerged rocks. The different colours mean different dangers. The buoys are bits of bamboo tied to sand-bags on the river bed. See that piece of tin fixed to the top of the bamboos? If we travel after dark you'll see what they are for.'

'Thank you, sir,' said Jyoti.

'And now leave the poor man alone,' Jean added.

The Belgian again protested that he didn't mind, but they were interrupted by a sound no-one wanted to hear. A drone above them signalled the appearance of an aircraft. It flew low overhead following the course of the river. Jean was no plane-spotter but she knew it had to be Japanese; they hadn't seen a British plane for weeks. The non-stop chatter from the deck area died, and 700 pairs of eyes followed the plane's progress. The nattering had begun to swell again when the plane returned, flying even lower.

'Hmm.' The Belgian compressed his lips. 'A reconnaissance flight. It would be no surprise if we travel only by night after this.'

'Would that be difficult?' Jean asked.

'These boats have searchlights.' He pointed to them. 'But it is more dangerous by night. It is easy to hit something in the darkness.'

The Belgian's words were prophetic. Not long afterwards a crew member toured the decks with a message for passengers. From now on the *Siam* would travel by night and lay up under cover during the daylight hours.

Sure enough after 6pm that evening the search-lights came on and the boat began negotiating the river under very different conditions. In darkness most of the passengers settled down on deck and fell asleep. There wasn't the slightest chance of Jyoti joining them. She stood at the rail with Jean to watch the new world unfold. It was a fantastical view designed by a deranged imagination. Deprived of the refugee chorus on the decks the scenes glided by in an unfamiliar silence.

What they saw under the searchlights was like a two-dimensional picture, with the river visible for a long way ahead. On either side the green of the landscape stood out starkly. The river sparkled with the bits of tin the Belgian had referred to and with the reflection of stars on the water and the phosphorescence of marine organisms in its depths. A stream of insects zipped through the air towards them, grotesquely magnified by the search-lights to the size of bats.

They saw frequent reminders of the dangers faced by any boat negotiating the river. Great uprooted tree trunks lolled in the shallows, along with the partly-seen wrecks of paddle-steamers scuttled by their owners or bombed by the Japanese. There was a moment when the pilot doused the lights, thinking a plane was overhead; a canoe materialised in the water ahead, the only clue to its existence the glowing tip of the oarsman's cheroot.

They stood at the rail for ages drinking in the spectacle. Jyoti's hand sought Jean's, and little gasps came from her as each new effect slid past. She stood on tiptoe and whispered in Jean's ear.

'Oh Jean, how good is this? I like this so much.'

'I know.' Jean put an arm round the girl's shoulders and pulled her close. She struggled to speak normally through a voice full of emotion. 'And as for you, my dear funny girl, I love *you* so much.'

Jean had always avoided trespassing on the mother-daughter relationship, and she felt a twinge of unease about Deepa, now fast asleep on the deck. But she'd denied her own feelings once that week and twice was more than she could handle.  For the first time in her life she felt she had real love to give.

The *Siam* arrived at Kalewa thirty-six hours later.  It was a small place and the small jetty was dwarfed by the mass of passengers pouring ashore.  Jean reflected that the town would never again see scenes like those of the Indian exodus.  However she was blithely unaware of developments in the military, and the way *their* plans were unravelling not very far south of Kalewa.  It would not be too long before she found out.

~ Nine ~

**The long walk from Kalewa**

As they left the jetty at Kalewa Jean turned to Deepa and Jyoti. 'This is it. We can't go further on the river and there are no vehicles. So we have to walk.'

'Then we walk, madam,' said Deepa in her low-key fashion.

'Yes we walk,' echoed Jyoti, marching ahead with a dramatic flinging of her arms.

Jean reckoned they'd been reasonably fortunate up to then. Two spells on the river interrupted by the strange interlude in Yenangyaung (convalescence, a battle, and an attachment to the army). But now came the hard bit. From her crude map she estimated it was 70 miles up the Kabaw Valley to Tamu, the first place of any consequence (and then not much), and another 30 to the much larger town of Imphal. She had no feel of the conditions they'd face on the way, except that Philip was one of several people who'd painted a horrendous picture of the valley. On the other hand the Dutch tea-planter had talked about the construction of a road, starting from Assam and extending into Burma. At what point they might pick up such a road was anyone's guess.

They were fairly well provisioned. The water bags were full and they expected to find streams en route. Thanks to gifts from her soldier friends they had a store of food, though it wouldn't take them all the way. (Someone once told her that Chinese coolies working on the Burma Road were given 60lb of rice to last 30 days, and amounts of this nature were well beyond their capacity to carry.) Sooner or later they would be reduced to 'living off the land'. Philip had always derided this concept; he said what it really meant was getting any food you could from villagers. And what they didn't know was whether the villages in this area would be friendly.

The first stretch of the journey was a hike to the small town of Kalemyo. To their surprise this went along a metalled road allowing good progress – except that it provided no protection from the burning sun. A Sikh walking alongside with his family overheard them talking about the surface.

'Be making most of pukka road, madam,' he told her. 'Road to Tamu big botheration, I am telling you.'

Many of their fellow refugees were travelling in parties – a couple of families, or as many as 50 people pulled together under a leader. More than once they'd been invited to join such a group, but politely declined. Large parties moved at the pace of their slowest member, and slow could be very slow. Already they'd passed a woman giving birth at the side of the road. Their plan was to get through the Kabaw Valley quickly, which they felt should be possible for three relatively fit females. The biggest worry was Jyoti; after all, she'd recently been through cholera and pneumonia and was unlikely to have reserves of stamina. Jean watched closely for any sign that the girl was flagging.

As the Sikh had foretold, the surface out of Kaleymo was very different from the metalled road – no more than a track and, though more or less level, very dusty. It would only have been suitable for vehicles during the dry season. Here at least the jungle – there was no other word for it – soared above their heads giving cover against the sun, but also precluding any chance of a breeze. The tangle of foliage, vines and creepers that shut out the sky soon exercised a claustrophobic effect upon them.

Hundreds of feet above, monkeys and blue-green parakeets set up an excited chattering, and they saw tree rats the size of squirrels scampering up and down the elongated trunks.

'One of those rats could make a decent meal for the three of us,' Jean remarked.

Jyoti pulled a disgusted expression. 'Oh Jean, *no*.'

'We may be glad of one,' Jean told her. 'You'd have to catch it, Jyoti, being as you're the youngest.'

Birds and mammals were as nothing compared to the insects that plagued them every inch of the way. It was too early in the day for the valley's notorious mosquitoes, but big black flies assailed their mouths and eyes, while small gnat-like creatures attacked their skin with pinprick bites. More acceptably, there were clouds of big yellow butterflies. Underfoot, inhabiting the carpet of leaf mould they walked upon, were ants and beetles and many tribes of insects beyond identification.

They quickly settled into a routine of resting for five minutes in every hour, a pattern that was to serve them for days into the future. If possible they timed the stops to coincide with one of the periodic jungle clearings, where sunlight filtered through the ceiling of foliage and redeemed the stifling atmosphere. They would rest for five minutes, drink a controlled ration of water, and move on.

The novelty of walking through jungle soon palled. Initially the trees exerted some fascination through their enormous, smooth-surfaced boles rising from an architectural tangle of roots. It was a surprise to find that many were hollow, something Jyoti had to be deterred from investigating because of the teeming animal and insect life that inhabited them. But after an hour or two they scarcely noticed these interminable ranks of colossi. Then their attention was more likely to be attracted by something unusual at the track-side. They passed a private car abandoned in good condition (with a child's toy left on the back seat) and then the skeleton of a large animal the size of a bullock.

More sinister sights were to follow. Three hours out of Kalewa they saw the first corpse, that of an elderly Indian man lying at the side of the track. The original impression of a body stretched out informally – as if the man had laid himself down for a snooze – was unexceptionable, until they noticed the ants. They walked on in subdued mood, which darkened further when the body of a child came into view. During the hours that followed the number of dead bodies multiplied and their distress at seeing them diminished. Soon they barely remarked upon such scenes and then they barely noticed them. Bodies became the natural order of things, casually left where they fell. Jean had seen plenty of hospital deaths – which nurse hadn't? – but never ones so randomly distributed and unmarked by the conventional obsequies.

It was now that she began to understand the extent of Burma's refugee tragedy and to see that that the death of troops in battle was merely the tip of a huge iceberg. She started thinking of the refugees who'd abandoned these bodies and how they must have felt. Then she thought of Jyoti and what it would be like leaving *her* behind in the jungle.

As Jean had hoped, the trio made good progress on the first day. They frequently passed groups of Indians on the track but were rarely overtaken in turn. They proceeded in contrasting ways that reflected their characters: Deepa in the restrained manner that she did everything else; Jyoti, seemingly unaffected by her illness, walking with a spring in her step, a rarity on the refugee trail. As for Jean herself she would almost have said – without admitting it to anyone – that she was enjoying the experience, rekindling her old enthusiasm for an extended physical challenge and discovering muscles that had been untested for years.

The day was tiring and supremely hot, but less traumatic than the Kabaw Valley's reputation suggested. In fact after Yenangyaung it struck her as a doddle. The most dramatic moment came late in the afternoon as they were thinking about calling a halt. From a distance away came the sound of something crashing through the jungle in their direction. The most likely explanation – a tank – was unpalatable because it would have been a Japanese tank. They stopped, hoping the thing – whatever it was – would pass harmlessly in front of them. Some hope. Suddenly the vegetation was violently displaced, dozens of birds shot from the trees and a full-grown elephant charged across their path trumpeting furiously, to disappear into the undergrowth. Where it had come from Jean couldn't begin to imagine. Jyoti, of course, was spellbound.

As soon as the next clearing materialised they stopped and cooked something to eat. All around them other groups of refugees were similarly employed. Now the mosquitoes came on the scene, as big and ugly as the Kabaw legends insisted. Jean was glad of the protection offered by her only pair of trousers, brought along as a last minute thought. The three women covered up every inch of bare skin, but the wretched creatures attacked their faces and hands without mercy. Jean hardly needed this reminder to take her Mecrapine pill, and was relieved to see Deepa making Jyoti swallow hers. After eating they put down their ground-sheets, erected mosquito nets on a crude system of sticks, and crawled underneath. The rigours of the day quickly took their toll. Jean remembered contemplating the outline of the moon through interlacing branches, then nothing more until waking the next morning.

The pattern of subsequent days walking through the valley held little variety. There was nowhere to go but the path and nothing on the path that had not been seen before. There was even a sameness about the refugees, because they saw nobody but Indians on the track.

Until the third day. For the first time since they'd started out the sound of an engine was heard, and before anyone could react an army jeep whizzed past them and disappeared into the distance. A couple of minutes later another one showed up. This time Jean had the presence of mind to call out 'Hello there'. The posh English accent intrigued the driver sufficiently for him to pull up down the track. Jean ran forward to meet him. The jeep was absolutely packed with British soldiers; you couldn't have levered another one in with a shoe horn.

'Are you *English*?' exclaimed a young army captain in the passenger seat.

'Military wife,' Jean said, 'Walking to India.'

'Bloody hell! Are you OK?'

'So far so good. But what about you? What on earth are you doing here?'

'You haven't heard?'

'Haven't heard what?'

'I suppose you wouldn't've. Silly of me. The British forces are retreating. Alexander gave the order on May 1st. Taking the same route as you, I expect.  We're the advance party, looking for a spot to set up our HQ.'

'Retreating!  But...' Jean couldn't get her head round it.  'You mean all of you?'

'The whole shoot.  We're giving Burma to the Japs.  Gift-wrapped.'

'And they're bleedin' welcome to it,' the driver added.

'Gosh!'

'We may come and take it back some day,' the captain went on. 'We'll have to see.  Look, I need to get a move on, lady.  Sorry we can't give you a lift.  You can see how we're fixed.'

'It's all right.  There are three of us anyway,' Jean said.  'Do you really think the troops can get through this way?'

'Good question.  Depends if the monsoon holds off.  With humidity like this it could start any day now and this track will become impassable.  Don't do a rain dance, whatever else you do.'

He was keen to move on but she got in a last question.  'When will the rest of you be along?'

'You'll see the eager beavers any time now,' he said.  'Though to tell the truth you girls look in better shape than most of our lot.  They've had enough.  They've had a bellyful.'

The jeep charged off, bouncing on the uneven ground.  Jean watched it go with mixed feelings.  Retreating from Burma!  The last three years of her life seemed to have been a waste of time.

'All for nothing, madam,' said Deepa, summing up Jean's feelings exactly.

Over the next three days the first waves of British troops began to overtake them on the track: vehicles first, then soldiers on foot, often with mules in attendance. The men were weary as hell but the mules looked worse. Jean was astonished some of them kept going at all. Loads had obviously been reduced to keep the beasts moving forwards.

She soon fell into conversation with a couple of privates, amazed – as the captain in the jeep had been – to find an Englishwoman in their midst. The two still had their rifles, but had jettisoned their packs for a couple of small shoulder bags each. One of them was a burly character well over six feet tall who hardly said a word. His friend, a gnarled little chap from east London called Bert, liked to talk.

'Do you know what's happening about the Japanese?' Jean asked him. 'We've not seen a sign of them since Yenangyaung.'

The little bloke recoiled. 'Gawd Mrs, don't mention them little bastards. Out of sight out of bleedin' mind, that's the way to do it. Can I offer you a fag?'

'Thank you very much but I don't smoke.'

'What about your friend here?'

Deepa grinned and shook her head. 'But that's nice of you,' said Jean. Her heart warmed to the little man for bringing Deepa into the picture. It was not something many British officers would have done.

'All the more for me then,' Bert said. 'Nah, we ain't seen none of them yeller perishers for days, thank the lord. Look Mrs, I ain't one of them military strategists but my sergeant, 'e thinks 'e is, bless 'is little heart, and 'e reckons the Japs 'ave lost interest after takin' Mandalay. Last *we* saw of 'em was at Monywa.'

'It seems odd though,' said Jean.

'Not really Mrs. I mean who'd bother with this load of crap, pardon my French. Ain't nuffink 'ere, is there. Just trees and more trees.'

'And more trees,' said his burly companion unexpectedly, speaking for the first time.

'This is Roger,' Bert said. "E says somefing about every three months. It's as well we *ain't* seen the Japs though,' he went on. 'We 'ad to leave our tanks and guns other side of the river. Our blokes 'ad a lot of fun blowin' em up. Like kids in a toyshop, they were.'

'What a waste,' said Jean.

'It's war, innit.'

They walked together for a while but the men had a quicker pace and she urged them to go ahead. 'We can catch up when you camp,' she said.

The three women continued on, but their speed had definitely slowed. Jean had bad blisters on both feet, giving her a lot of pain; no question of 'enjoying' the walking experience now. Deepa's feet were OK but she struggled all the same, uncomplainingly, as went without saying. Jyoti was now the best walker of the three but even she wasn't herself and, when pressed, admitted that her eyes hurt.

Now they were frequently overtaken by groups of soldiers on foot and there was the usual banter at the discovery of an Englishwoman in the jungle. Only at this point did it occur to Jean that Philip might turn up here. It shocked her that she'd not been keeping an eye open for the man who was, after all, her husband. She could at least have asked after him but – she realised with shame – the person she really wanted news of was Bruce. To punish herself she refrained from talking about either of them.

By now their original notion of making rapid progress to Tamu was a distant dream. They concentrated on putting one foot in front of the other, heads down, saying little. With the arrival of British forces the trail was impossibly congested. The count of dead bodies along the way reached alarming proportions. Refugees had been indisciplined in their toilet habits and the results were piled up everywhere. The smell of death and ordure was a constant accompaniment to the journey. The ceiling of giant trees obliterated the light and depressed their spirits. They longed to be back in open country and regain a sense of freedom.

Jean's lips were cracked and bleeding like everyone else's. She could hardly conceive of heat and humidity rising higher. It was a surprise when an unfamiliar pattering sound came from the tree-tops and and large raindrops filtered through the leafy canopy to dampen their clothing.

'It's rain madam,' said Deepa.

'Rain!' cried Jyoti.

'Rain!' came the cry from refugees and soldiers all along the line.

The sense of relief was misplaced. The last thing they needed was a downpour, which would turn the track into a quagmire. Fortunately the rain was short-lived. 'It's a mango shower,' said Jean, remembering a phrase she'd heard about rain that preceded the mango crop – mangoes which still remained infuriatingly too hard to eat. The shower laid the dust but had another, highly undesirable outcome. Leeches, until then an occasional problem, became a rampant menace, emerging from the damp ground to invade every part of their bodies. Now when the women stopped to rest their first task was to find these ghoulish creatures. They were an inch to three inches long and had to be removed by scraping with a knife or applying salt (or a lighted fag-end if they'd had one). They left behind small punctures which were slow to heal.

More by luck than judgement the women renewed contact that evening with the two army privates. They camped nearby and ate with them companionably. Bert, the gnarled little chap, fussed around his burly companion in a way that reminded Jean of the two friends in John Steinbeck's novel, *Of mice and men*, which she'd read in Rangoon.

'I'm worried about Roger,' he confided to Jean over the evening meal. 'E don't complain but I know 'is eyes are killing 'im. I know 'im, see.'

'Roger too!' exclaimed Jean.

'Eh?'

'Sorry Bert, I didn't explain. It's just that Jyoti has eye problems as well.'

'Go on! What can it mean Mrs, you bein' a nurse an' all?'

Jean shook her head. 'I wish I knew.' Suddenly she leapt to her feet. 'Of course, how stupid of me. Mangoes!'

'I beg your pudding?'

'Just thinking aloud. Let me see – *could* it be that, I wonder.' He waited while she thought it through. 'The matron I worked with in Rangoon told me,' she explained. 'We're nearly in the mango season, and when you get those showers of rain you also get things they call mango flies.'

'Get away.'

'Tiny, tiny things, like black spots.'

'I seen 'em,' cried Bert, 'Clouds of 'em dancin' in front of me eyes. But wot's that got to do wiv...'

'Hold on Bert and I'll tell you. These things have a nasty habit – they like to lay their eggs under people's eye-lids.'

'The little buggers.'

'And when the eggs hatch...well, it causes all sorts of trouble.  We're talking conjunctivitis or worse.  The trouble is, how to deal with it in the middle of a jungle?  Wait a minute.' She made a grab for her bag and rummaged through the medical kit that Matron had given her.  'Let me check...just in case...now then, what's this?'

She pulled out a phial of liquid and peered at the label in the moonlight.  Deepa peered with her.

'What is it, madam?'

'Eye drops!  Matron, you amazing woman,' Jean cried, kissing the phial.  'You wonderful, kind, wise, curmudgeonly, clairvoyant old bat. Jyoti, lie back with your head on your mother's lap and hold your left eye open.  We're going to make you feel better.'

She put drops into Jyoti's eyes, did the same for Roger, and told them she'd repeat the dose twice in the morning.  Medicine can be so simple, she thought, if only you know what you're doing.   Next day the five of them walked together, separating after lunch with mutual expressions of goodwill.  Both patients said their eyes felt better.

By now the people walking the track were spread out in little bunches, and it was possible to travel for short periods without seeing anyone else at all.  Not all those they met were as agreeable as Bert and Roger.  The regular soldiers were friendly, but their ranks were interspersed with batches of deserters who gave a very different impression.  According to Bert you could always tell deserters because they'd abandoned their rifles.  These men were aggressive, drunken (if they could get hold of liquor), thieving, and prone to violence.

Apart from the military there were still large numbers of Indian refugees on the track, many of them ill or in a desperate condition. Cases of malaria, cholera and dysentery were common.

Perhaps the biggest danger en route came from gangs of Burmans, whose allegiances at this stage of the war could never be taken for granted. Many had deserted, from the British army or the Japanese. Jean's little group came close to a nasty incident when they strayed from the path looking for coconuts to supplement their provisions. Three dubious-looking Burmans had sprung from the bushes demanding to know what the women were doing there. They carried *dahs* and looked ready to use them. At such moments a knowledge of the language was an asset. Deepa and Jyoti struck up a conversation, suppressing their fear and trying to behave naturally. The Burmans backed off and even showed them where to find a patch of wild strawberries.

At this point in the journey it was obvious that the women's progress had slowed alarmingly. Jyoti's eyes no longer troubled her but the other two were struggling. Jean silently cursed that they were never all fit at the same time. As usual she and Deepa competed with each other to deny that anything was wrong.

'Deepa, what's the problem?' Jean asked, labouring along the path beside her friend. 'You're not feeling well, are you? I can see you're not.'

Deepa roused herself to adopt one of her insouciant airs. 'Oh yes and madam, of course, she is feeling *very* well.'

'Not *very* well,' Jean admitted.

'No, not very well at all. Let me see madam's feet.'

'My feet are fine.'

Deepa stopped abruptly and sat down at the side of the track. 'Not going further unless madam shows me her feet.'

'Oh really Deepa, don't make such a fuss.'

Nonetheless Jean stopped and removed her shoes and socks. The feet thus revealed were a truly disgusting sight, worse than even she had realised. The blisters had become infected and the result was a swollen, suppurating mess.

She gave an unconvincing shrug. 'Well there's nothing to be done about it. We just go on.'

'No.' Deepa was inspecting the damage more closely. 'Not possible madam walk on these. We rest until feet are better.'

'Deepa, we can't hang around in this ghastly valley. Let's wait till we get up in the hills at least.'

'Next village,' Deepa said in a tone that brooked no refusal. 'They have local medicines.'

Sure enough Deepa stopped at the next Naga village and asked to see the headman. He took them to a filthy hut in the jungle, where a wizened old man inspected Jean's feet. He gave his verdict via the headman, who translated the Naga dialect into Burmese.

'He says he will wrap up your feet using a special medicine,' Deepa reported back. 'You must keep this in place all night.'

'I don't know,' Jean said doubtfully. She imagined it would all go wrong; that she would never walk again, would die immolated in the Kabaw Valley.

Deepa was implacable. 'You will do it.'

'I'll hold your hand, Jean,' Jyoti offered.

The wizened man spent ten minutes in his hut mixing different potions together. Then he smeared a thick green paste all over Jean's feet and wrapped it round with banana leaves. The other two looked on.

'What's this stuff made of?' said Jean.

'Do not ask,' insisted Deepa.

'It's a nice colour,' said Jyoti.

The witch-doctor – as Jean thought of him – spoke again to the headman.

'He says it will be very painful in the night,' Deepa translated, but in the morning your feet will be much better.'

As the man had predicted, Jean spent an extremely uncomfortable night camping in the village. She longed to rip the monstrous poultice from her feet but the thought of Deepa's reaction deterred her. Eventually she slept, and in the morning her feet were remarkably transformed. They hurt a bit but she felt like a new woman. When they said goodbye the witch-doctor wouldn't accept money but extracted a pink blouse from her as payment.

The village was a little off the beaten track, and as they set out again three British soldiers fell in behind them. That they were dirty and unshaven was nothing unusual in the Kabaw Valley but something about the men put Jean on her guard, perhaps because (Bert's acid test for deserters) they were not carrying rifles. It was hard to imagine what they were doing there unless it was buying food from the villagers, or more likely, stealing it.

The men advanced until they were a couple of yards behind. Instead of passing they remained on the women's heels. Unusually they gave no greeting but began swapping ribald comments and guffaws. If they weren't drunk, they certainly sounded like it.

'What have we got here, boys?  Looks like three ladies asking for trouble.'

'If they want trouble we can give it to them.'

'Three of them and three of us.  Ain't that considerate.'

'Any preferences, Jed?  The little one looks nice.  Or what about the white woman?'

Not that scrawny cow,' said the Jed character.  'I'll take the other one. It's been months since I've had any dark meat.  Yes I mean you, darling – don't look round, will you.'

Barely a yard separated the two groups and the men's proximity ratcheted up the air of menace.  The suddenness of the danger took Jean's breath away.  She made up her mind, drawing Deepa and Jyoti to one side and turning to face their persecutors.  Her heart was pounding like mad.

'You men go on your way,' she told them, trying to keep her voice level, 'And don't bother us.'

'Oh don't bother us,' said a man with a blood-shot eye, imitating Jean's accent.  'Ain't she the hoity-toity little madam.'

The one they called Jed approached to within inches of Jean, towering above her.  She smelt his foul breath as he spoke in barely a whisper.

'Listen to me, you arrogant little bitch.  You don't tell *us* what to do. We'll bother you all right, and when we've finished you'll be grateful for it.'

She thought about shouting for help but it was futile; they were too far from the track.  Any comment would be pointless but she was determined to make one anyway.  Above all she wanted to draw attention away from Deepa and Jyoti.

'What a privilege it will be,' she said in a sneering tone that even she was repelled by. 'I thrill to the thought of your touch. Three filthy deserters, the lowest scum in the British army.'

She didn't actually see him lash out but found she was on the ground, head buzzing, tasting blood. It was only at this point that she remembered Philip's revolver. Her eyes were refusing to focus properly but she made out the Jed person grappling with Deepa. Then she saw Jyoti run forward to pummel Jed with her little fists until the bloodshot eye man intervened, hurling the girl to the ground. He wasn't to know it but that action sealed his fate.

Deepa was the last woman for hysterics, whatever the situation. Wrestling with Jed she clawed at his throat, then said something in Hindi and spat in his face. As he tried to rip her clothes she put a knee into his groin, making him double up in pain.

The other two guffawed, until they saw Jed's expression; he was beside himself, furious beyond all reason. He limped towards Deepa, biting out words, saliva spraying from his lips.

'You'll...be...sorry.'

'Stop where you are,' Jean shouted, spitting out blood. He looked up to see 'the white woman' kneeling on the ground pointing a .45 revolver.

'I'm warning you, I want to use this,' Jean cried. 'I mean I *really* want to use it. Take one more step and I will.'

Jed roared with laughter. 'You silly bitch. You won't shoot and you know it. And if you did you'd miss by a mile. Give me that toy.'

He reached a hand out and took a step towards her. Jean pulled the trigger.  The noise sent dozens of birds scattering from the trees.

'She shot me.'  Jed spoke in a puzzled, falsetto voice.  His legs folded, sending him sluggishly to the ground.

'I told you,' Jean said.

The other two froze, making no move to assist their fallen comrade.

Jean had shot living things before, notably game birds in India, but never a human being.  It surprised her that she'd stayed so calm.  Even now her hands were steady.  What this said about her character she didn't know, and at that moment she didn't care.

Jyoti's body had lain still since the moment she was thrown to the ground.  Now she made an effort to sit up.  The movement reminded Jean of unfinished business and she fired again.  The bloodshot eye man croaked and fell, holding his stomach.  She hoped his death would be long and painful.  The third man turned to run and she let him go.

She joined Deepa, who was kneeling by her daughter.

'Is she all right?'

'All right, madam.'

'I'm all right,' Jyoti piped up.

They knelt on the ground with their arms around each other.

'Thank god you're all right,' Jean said.  'And your amazing mother – what a wildcat she is.'

Deepa cast a scornful eye on the two bodies.  'Men like that – they are nothing.'

A reaction had set in and Jean was trembling uncontrollably.  The three women stayed down in a close embrace.  Naga tribesmen had come onto the scene, gathering in a respectful circle to watch in silence.

Afterwards they walked, and later in the day Jean saw the first signs of road  construction.  The Indian government had bulldozers churning up the land  and hundreds of Chinese coolies doing manual tasks.  The trail remained rough but it seemed likely that refugees who had ventured that far would now find the going easier.  Whether the work had been started in time was another matter.  Any number of hazards remained, the monsoon was imminent, and the Indians now passing through – swamped by British troops – were weaker and slower than their predecessors.

The following day Jean's party reached Tamu.  They'd been aiming so long at this place, the first name on the Kabaw Valley map, that arrival there proved a sad disappointment.  Tamu was a village: a clearing in the jungle, a post office, a police station, a small hospital – and a makeshift camp bursting at the seams with desperate refugees.  It was the most depressing place Jean had seen.  Hundreds of sick and starving people lay inertly under canvas.  Others stumbled through the village with hands extended in supplication, or haggled with Naga tribesmen for wildly overpriced provisions.  The few examples of kindness she saw were outweighed by boorish or bestial behaviour.  To have involved herself in the many individual tragedies would, Jean knew, be like signing her own death sentence.  Even so the sight of a small child trying to feed rice to its dying mother overcame her resolve, and she took time showing the infant to relief workers.

Against Deepa's wishes she insisted they join the long queue for treatment at the hospital.  A group of overworked nurses – oh how she identified with them! – did their best to alleviate the tidal wave of suffering.  One batch stood in a line inoculating people against cholera.

When it came to their own turn a nurse quickly confirmed that Deepa was suffering from malaria. She offered a supply of Mecrapine and Deepa surprised Jean by accepting.

'I'm sorry Jean,' she said with an embarrassed sideways glance. 'I lost a lot of tablets in the jungle, I don't know how.'

Jean saw immediately what had happened. 'So you gave all your tablets to Jyoti. Oh Deepa, if only you'd said, I'd have given you some of mine.'

Deepa shook her head. 'Of course no. It was my fault. I like to make sacrifice.'

There was some truth in that, Jean thought. Deepa was inured to a life of sacrifice and self-denial, even took a grim pleasure in such things. It was part of her charm.

As they turned to go the nurse drew Jean aside. 'Look, you're a nurse yourself. You know the scene. Mecrapine isn't everything – you can take the stuff and still contract malaria – but it'll be hard for your friend to kick the condition now.'

Jean didn't want to ask but she had to. 'What are you telling me? Do you think it's really bad?'

'She has all the signs of cerebral malaria. I'm amazed she's made it this far.'

Jean began to cry and found she couldn't stop. The nurse took her arm.

'I'm sorry. She seems very nice.'

'I knew really,' Jean snivelled between sobs. 'I thought...I hoped...a miracle.' She wiped a sleeve across her eyes. 'We'll rest up here a while – see if she can regain some strength.'

The nurse shook her head. 'I wouldn't do that. You have the

youngster to think of. This place drags people down. It's become somewhere to die.'

'Then what?'

The woman shrugged helplessly. 'What everyone else is doing. They walk till they drop. It's what this awful business has been from the beginning.'

If there were doubts left in Jean's mind, Deepa herself resolved them. She refused to contemplate staying in Tamu for any time at all.

'Bad place madam.'

'But it will be so hard for you,' Jean said.

Deepa's shrug echoed the nurse's. 'I know.'

On the three of them went, relieved to leave Tamu behind. And three miles down the road they found a more upbeat unit, a roadside outpost set up by the Indian Tea Association. It was the type of facility described by Jan, the Dutch tea-planter they'd met on the paddle-steamer out of Prome. Here were medical facilities, a supply of clean water, and food parcels: parcels of rice, bully beef, tea, sugar, salt, and dried fruit, the latter especially welcome as it could be eaten raw. The atmosphere was entirely different from Tamu and gave Jean the feeling that, at last, help was at hand. As she talked to one of the officials a voice came from behind her – 'Jean, is it really you?' – and she wheeled round to find the Dutch planter standing there with a broad smile on his face and a hand held out in greeting.

'Jan!' She was enormously pleased to see him. 'It was you who told me about these camps and here you are! I can't believe it.'

In a glance he took in Jean's companions: Deepa sitting by the roadside to rest, and Jyoti excitedly examining the contents of a parcel.

'The little girl seems much better than when I last saw her, but...' He lowered his voice. 'Her mother doesn't look at all good.'

'She isn't.' Jean outlined Deepa's condition.

He shook his head. 'It's the Kabaw Valley. It's a killer. You know Jean, I've seen this a thousand times and I still can't get used to it. Look, why don't you three stay here tonight. We can give Deepa somewhere to rest.' He dropped his voice again. 'And don't shout it about, but we've got lizard to eat. It's a delicacy in these parts.'

'Oh Jan.' She stood on tiptoe and kissed him. She knew he liked her and tried not to take advantage of it but dammit, *she* liked *him*. 'Thank you. Thank you. I told you before, you're my guardian angel.'

Late that evening, when Deepa and Jyoti were sleeping, they sat in Jan's tent and talked. Coils were burning to keep the mosquitoes at bay. The sounds of camp activity filtered in through the canvas. With roast lizard inside her Jean almost felt optimistic. Jan soon brought her back to earth.

'I'm afraid you've got the hills ahead. It won't be easy, you know. They're steep, and believe it or not they get really cold at night.'

'Is there anything I can do for Deepa?' she asked.

He met her eyes with a grim face. 'Yes. Look after her daughter.'

'I see.'

'I'm sorry, Jean.'

'No Jan, you've been wonderful.' He was the second person to rule out hope and she'd begun to believe them. 'Are people always in such a desperate state here?' she asked. 'Haven't things improved at all since you started?'

'I don't know about improved. They've changed. The early refugees brought absurd amounts of luggage, and they had the cash to pay high rates for Naga porters. It didn't stop them from dying on the trail. Now...' He spread his hands helplessly. 'You see what it's like. People just have the clothes they stand up in. I reckon two in three of them are ill.' He thought for a moment. 'With a few exceptions. You may have seen the convoy that went past this afternoon.'

'I did,' said Jean. 'What was that about?'

'Burma Oil Company, getting their Eurasian staff out in style. It's caused a lot of ill-feeling because the Indian employees are left to fend for themselves.' He shrugged. 'I suppose everyone takes advantage of an inside track, if there is one.'

'In the way that I've let you help me,' she said quietly.

He smiled. 'That's how it is, Jean.'

They sat in silence for a while. Insects flitted round the oil lamp, throwing grotesque shadows onto the canvas.

'One thing may help you,' he said eventually. 'It should be firmer going under foot from here on. There'll be people working on the road all the way to Imphal, and then on to Dimapur. It keeps those wretched leeches down too.'

'Hard to believe you've built a road so quickly,' she said, 'Through all that jungle.'

'It got top priority once they decided the troops were coming out this way. And of course there's also the thought...'

'What?'

He flashed a quirky smile. 'Who knows? That one day the military will come back down it the other way. Take Burma back again.'

Jean thought of all the devastation she'd seen, the bombing of cities and overflowing hospitals, the scuttled paddle-steamers, the bodies piled up at the roadsides and bobbing in the river.

'Poor Burma.'

'I entirely agree with you,' the planter said.

Jean rose early the next morning and took a walk round the camp. Already droves of military and civilians were moving along the road. According to Jan, General Alexander had ordered troops to help with evacuating civilians wherever possible and 'without class distinction'. But that assumed the presence of vehicles, and around Tamu most people were on foot, stumbling onwards, carrying the few scraps of belongings they could manage plus, in the case of most soldiers, their rifles. Here the military outnumbered refugees two to one, bossing the right of way and hogging the lion's share of provisions. In spite of it their general condition seemed little better than that of the Indians.

Some troops had enough energy over left for dodges – the sort of dodges that were the province of soldiers everywhere. A British NCO had set up a roadside stall equipped with betting slips and bunches of rupees, and men of all ranks bet on propositions about the retreat. The most popular wager concerned the number of brigadiers passing through Tamu each day. The NCO's opinion of officers was clear, and Jean didn't reveal that she was married to one of the breed.

Deepa was on her feet early, a little refreshed from spending a comfortable night, and she insisted they move on. Before that Jean had the unhappy task of saying goodbye to Jan. She was comfortable in his company and for a few brief hours she'd even felt safe. They exchanged standby addresses – something more tangible, at least, than 'an outpost in the jungle' – but she had the feeling they'd never meet again. She suspected that if she did get in touch he would press her to marry him, existing husband notwithstanding. Her personal life had never been so complicated.

As soon as the road climbed into the hills Deepa began to struggle. She forced herself on with remarkable tenacity but their pace slowed to a crawl. The trail that rose inexorably before them was flinty, flanked by very tall grasses and the occasional stunted tree. The Dutchman had spoken of highs reaching five thousand feet and more, and Jean couldn't even fantasise about Deepa handling such conditions. The past few days had been a story of her unremitting decline. At some point, without Jean noticing it, the unacceptable had merged into the inevitable. It seemed pointless to continue yet they trudged on; 'People walk till they drop,' the nurse had said. There was irony in this because, for the first time since they'd started, the insignia of civilisation were all around – Tea Association camps, officials on the trail, bulldozers wheeling back and forth. Yet none of it redeemed the hundreds of refugees lying down to die at the side of the track. Now Jean understood the awful apathy that could descend. They passed an official pleading with a family of Indians to get up and walk. The father lay listlessly between his wife and a teenage daughter, ignoring the man's promptings. 'Leave us,' Jean heard him say, 'We will die here.'

When they stopped for one of their increasingly frequent rests, Deepa drew Jean aside.

'It is time, madam.'

Jean stared at her wildly. 'What do you mean, it's time?'

'Leave me here. I can't do this. You know I can't.'

'Don't be ridiculous, Deepa.'

'It's no good, madam.  Please, you go.  Take Jyoti and keep her safe. *Please*.'

'Oh and if I was ill, *you'd* go off and leave me, wouldn't you?  Just like that.'

'Of course I would.'  Deepa mustered an airy shrug.  'Just like that.  I think "End of madam, no-good white woman.  Leave her.  Easy!".'

Deepa's eyes, deep in their hollowed-out sockets, blazed with the animation that had deserted her body.  By some trick of nature she looked more beautiful than ever.  A great sadness descended on Jean. She clasped the woman in her arms and whispered 'Deepa, you are such a big, big liar.  I am *not* leaving you behind, do you hear.  We'll get there together if I have to drag you every inch of the way.  Do you hear me?'

'I must do as my mistress orders,' Deepa said demurely.

'Yes,' Jean said.  'You'd better believe it.'

On one of their rest stops Jean had a piece of luck.  She'd gone off into the long undergrowth for a pee, which she always did with trepidation because of Burma's reputation for snakes (not one of which had they seen).  As she squatted down, her eye was caught by the sun gleaming from something metallic.  She went to investigate, again with the greatest caution, and discovered a metal tube fixed to a frame that was in turn attached to wheels.  A bicycle!  A special kind of bicycle with solid rubber tyres.  She dragged the thing onto the road, albeit with no great expectations, only to find it was in working order.  What it was doing there she couldn't imagine.  She knew Japanese scouts used bikes to negotiate the jungle, but British military intelligence said the Japs had never penetrated this far north.  Well, it seemed that military intelligence was wrong.

The vehicle had panniers either side of its rear wheel and Jean distributed all their belongings into them. In a sense this made their progress easier, because Jean had been carrying most of Deepa's things as well as her own, and even Jyoti had stuffed the stove into her bag along with Herbert. Jean made the saddle more comfortable by strapping a blanket round it, then asked Deepa to sit on the refashioned seat with her feet on the pedals.

'Is it OK?' she asked.

'It's good madam – but I don't know how to ride bike.'

'And you're not going to ride this one, you daft ha'p'orth. I'm going to push you.'

Ignoring Deepa's protests, she essayed a trial run over the next stretch of trail. It went most smoothly when Deepa put an arm over Jean's shoulders and Jyoti pushed the handlebar on the other side. They were a strange sight (reminding Jean of the three-legged race at school sports days) and other refugees cast curious glances in their direction. On level ground progress was actually quicker, but of course going up-hill put a tremendous strain on Jean's legs. She noticed that Deepa leaned upon her more and more heavily. The discovery of the bike had not come a moment too soon.

They called a halt earlier than usual that evening because both women were exhausted. It was Jyoti who prepared something to eat as the other two sat around listlessly. Deepa ate almost nothing. As Jan had warned, the night-time temperature dropped alarmingly, and even with most of their clothes on the women shivered. Another pre-monsoon shower had come down, reviving the leeches and further lowering their own spirits. It didn't help that shortly before stopping they'd passed a most depressing sight: the corpses of three middle-aged women lying together on the road, dressed – in a futile bid for warmth – in their finest clothes.

Immediately after eating Jean had laid her body on the ground, too tired for anything but sleep, yet a deep sense of unease inhibited her from losing consciousness. A few yards away Deepa and Jyoti lay close together. Deepa was murmuring hypnotically in a low, unbroken stream of Hindi. She was rarely a demonstrative mother but on this night she clasped Jyoti to her breast stroking her hair over and over again. That was the image in Jean's eyes as she at last fell asleep.

The morning dawned as cheerless as the night before. They drank some tea, then Jean and Jyoti packed up their pathetic belongings and helped Deepa onto the bike. She fell like a dead weight on Jean's shoulders. Jean forced her stiff legs to move and away they went, creeping up the hillside.

After two hours on the road Deepa said 'Stop here, madam.'

'Are you sure?' Jean queried. 'I could go a bit further before we rest.'

'No madam. Meaning stop, last stop.'

Jean did stop, still puzzled, and Jyoti came round the bike to help her mother off. They half carried her to the side of the road and Jyoti laid down ground-sheets and blankets to make a comfortable place. Deepa sank back with her head on one of the panniers and Jyoti signalled Jean to sit beside her mother.

Deepa was smiling. 'Come near me, Jean.'

Jean began to cry. So many times on the journey had she urged Deepa to use her first name, and hearing it spoken now brought home the compelling truth. Of all people, she should have known; in the hospital she'd frequently observed that patients knew when they were going to die. Deepa and Jyoti knew because that had been settled during the night.

Deepa took her hand. 'Don't cry Jean.'

'Of course I'm crying,' Jean said, weeping bitterly, all pretence at an end. 'You're my dear, dear friend. Of course I'm crying.'

'There is nothing more I want,' Deepa went on. 'When I am your maid in Rangoon I think, maybe madam very nice person, and I find it is true. These weeks on our journey, it is a happy time.'

'Oh stop it, Deepa. I can't bear it.'

The sick woman raised herself slightly on the pannier. 'I want to ask something. Please Jean, *please* look after Jyoti for me.'

'Of course. Of course I will. I have your sister's address in India and I'll make sure she gets there.'

'No.' Deepa gripped her hand with surprising force. 'Not my sister. Husband not good man. Jyoti likes *you*. You know she does.'

'Oh god, Deepa.' There was a moral issue about family that neither of them was in a state to grapple with. 'You know I would love to be with Jyoti. Look, I will go to your sister and talk to her. I promise.'

The response was muffled and she realised that Deepa could no longer see or hear clearly. Jean squeezed her hand and got to her feet. She gestured to Jyoti, who knelt beside her mother.

It took Deepa half an hour to die, so finely had she judged her last moments. Jean sat with an arm round Jyoti until it was over. Passing Indians looked at them incuriously, for this kind of scene was commonplace.

Jean found Jyoti's demeanour astonishing. Perhaps it was that Indian custom of familiarising children with death, for she could not imagine a British child showing such calm acceptance. Even so, she remembered something Jyoti had said after seeing her father's skull smashed on the funeral pyre: 'His soul has flown free from his body'. Out here the usual funeral obsequies were inconceivable, as they had been for thousands of Indians who'd died on the trail to Assam. It would be as much as Jean could do to drag Deepa's body into the undergrowth. Jyoti would not make a fuss, for the girl bore every adversity with fortitude. But there had to be a breaking point for even this remarkable young woman.

A familiar voice broke into Jean's reverie. 'Now then Mrs, wot's goin' on 'ere?'

She looked up to see Bert and Roger on the road, together with two other soldiers. Jean thought, this is my karma: at every crisis along the way men of goodwill magically materialise.

Explanations were made. The two Cockneys had fallen behind when Bert suffered a bout of malaria, but – 'I'm feelin' more chipper now, Mrs.' The trouble with Roger's eyes had cleared up completely. Jean gave them a run-down from her side. There was no need to convey the tragic news for Jyoti was at the road-side by her mother's body. But she did ask if the men would help her move Deepa off the track. When she mentioned the impossibility of arranging an Indian funeral, Bert pressed her for more details.

'Well then, Mrs,' Bert said after he'd absorbed the information, 'It ain't that 'ard to manage, surely?'

Jean shook her head. 'It's just not possible out here, Bert.'

'Now you 'old on.' He had a word with the other men, who were standing at a respectful distance. 'I got an idea, Mrs,' he said. 'D'you mind if we 'ave a look-see? Spy out the lie of the land, so to speak.'

'I don't understand,' she said.

'No Mrs. You leave it to us.'

He collected the others, quite the organiser, and they went off into the long grass. They were back in half an hour looking pleased with themselves.

'Goin' well, Mrs,' Bert said. 'There's just one more fing wot would 'elp and...' He listened intently, then raised his eyes to the horizon. 'Blow me if it ain't turning up right now.'

He broke away to flag down the army jeep that was coming down the trail crammed with soldiers. Jean witnessed an earnest conversation with the officer, followed by an exchange of goods: Bert handing over a packet of cigarettes and receiving (a poor exchange, Jean thought) a battered tin can.

'Now if you ladies would like to follow us,' he said, returning to Jean's side. With surprising delicacy he arranged for the men gently to raise Deepa's body between them and march in slow motion into the long grass. He asked Jyoti if she would walk alongside holding her mother's hand. Jean followed in a daze.

After a few minutes they stopped beside the trunk of a fallen tree, a gnarled, ancient affair some six feet long, upon which the men had heaped a big pile of bracken gathered from the surrounding terrain. With great ceremony they lowered Deepa's body on top of it. Bert handed Jyoti a thick length of bamboo.

'I bin told wot' you 'ave to do wiv this miss and it can't be easy, so maybe you can get your Mrs to help you?'

'Thank you Mr Bert, I will,' said Jyoti, responding in kind to the soldier's formality.

'And listen miss, we ain't never done this before, so please try and forgive any bits we get wrong, eh?'

'I will, Mr Bert.'

With this Bert poured the contents of the can – which contained paraffin – through various interstices along the length of the battered tree trunk, then lit a match.

'And may I suggest, ladies, you stand well back, 'cos this trunk is a bit hollow, like, and I ain't got no idea wot might be inside it.'

It was as well that Bert made this last suggestion. As he dropped the lighted match into the trunk's ragged interior there was a tremendous 'whoosh' and flames leapt six feet high, projecting a fierce heat. Almost at once a panorama of Burmese insect life was catapulted into the air, some of it burning brightly, while rats and other small mammals scuttled from the trunk's ends followed by three snakes which had been sharing the premises in apparent harmony. Meanwhile the four soldiers, stationed at regular intervals round the pyre, snapped to attention with shouldered rifles and stood unmoving and expressionless. Jean could only marvel at the mixture of Indian and British-military ceremonial cooked up by Bert's quirky imagination.

She could scarcely bear to look at Deepa's body being consumed by the flames, but Jyoti had no such reservations. Fire was a central component of Indian death and the girl stood by impassively with the bamboo pole at her side.

'You say when to do it, Jyoti,' Jean murmured.

Bert and his mates stayed stiffly motionless for what seemed a long time until Jyoti said the word. She and Jean went forward, centred the bamboo on the smouldering remains of the forehead, and struck down together as hard as they could. Jean knew from the cracking sound and Jyoti's little sigh of relief that the job was done. Bert muttered a low command and the men lowered their rifles to stand easy.

Jyoti walked forward. 'Mr Bert?'

'Yes miss.'

'There were no bits wrong, Mr Bert. Everything was right. It was the most right thing it could have been.'

'Thank you, miss. Very kind of you.'

They left Deepa's remains where they stood and Jean thanked the men, though no thanks could have been sufficient. Before they parted she persuaded them to take away some small items of food. Later she reflected that of the thousands of deaths on the route to India, only one could have been marked in such a signal manner.

When Jean and Jyoti set off again their progress was very different. They abandoned the bicycle and went on foot. It was strange to be walking as a couple rather than a trio, but of course they moved faster. They were both fit. Blisters had healed and their feet were hardened by walking long distances. They had no medical issues beyond the fungal infections that afflicted their skin, as happened to so many people on the trail. They tramped on side by side at a steady pace that took them past refugees and soldiers alike.

Jyoti moved with a very upright stance, staring straight ahead, saying little but occasionally taking Jean's hand for short distances. From time to time Jean stole sideways glances. Her concern for the girl was emotional rather than physical. She had been through so much, yet showed few overt signs of it. She was quieter than usual and had taken to walking with Herbert in her arms for long periods, but that was all. She didn't cry. For that matter Jean couldn't ever remember tears; when upset, Jyoti's reaction was to take refuge in silence. Yet Jean knew from hospital experience that bottling up grief could lead to dire consequences: illnesses like jaundice, or a serious infection from a minor injury, even a scratch.

When they stopped to rest, she resolved to broach the subject. She waited until they'd finished eating the usual dollop of boiled rice.

'How are you, Jyoti? How do you feel today?'

'It's all right, Jean.'

'You must be thinking a lot about your mother.'

'I do think of her, of course.'

The girl was sitting cross-legged on the ground-sheet with Herbert in her lap. She looked pale but composed; not deliberately uncommunicative but more introspective than usual. Jean racked her brains to think of a way to get through. She remembered Deepa saying 'Sometimes *I* don't know what she's thinking.'

'I can't imagine how you're feeling,' she said. 'My own mother is still alive. I just know you must be terribly upset.'

Jyoti said nothing.

'You know, it's perfectly all right if...I mean, if you feel like crying, well it can be good for you.' Still the girl said nothing. 'Sometimes,' Jean pressed on desperately, 'People say it's bad for you *not* to cry.'

'It's all right Jean,' Jyoti repeated, this time with an air of finality.

Jean had to let it go. A barrier had come between them and she didn't know how to overcome it. She'd often enough found words of condolence for the relatives of hospital patients, but they had no place here. It struck her that she didn't really know Jyoti well; that their relationship, though intense, had been brief.

As they approached the town of Palel the next day the road was covered with a fine white dust. There was no shade and the extreme heat had returned. Even on Palel's outskirts they could see that this was a more substantial place than Tamu. The local houses, situated under mango trees, were built of bamboo on a mud foundation and had two steps up to the doors. The womenfolk wore colourful striped shirts.

They were tired after a long day and Jean was about to suggest a rest when Jyoti stopped abruptly in the middle of the road.

'Herbert!'

She was turning her bag inside out, looking highly agitated.

'What is it, Jyoti?'

'It's Herbert. I've lost him.'

'Oh no! Think back. Can you remember where?'

'Yes Jean, I know. The big rock by the side of the road, where we stopped for a drink. I put him on the rock.'

Jean remembered. It had to be at least five miles back.

'Oh Jyoti,' she said again.

'It's all right,' the girl said. 'I know we must go on. Perhaps someone else will find Herbert and look after him. It can't be helped.'

*Five miles*, Jean was thinking. Five miles there and five miles back, all for a bear that someone else will have picked up.

They walked on for a few minutes, doing the sensible thing, but it was no use. Jean put a restraining hand on Jyoti's shoulder.

'We're going the wrong way.'

The girl looked up at her.

'Let's go back.'

For the first time since Deepa's death, Jyoti smiled. 'I'm sorry, Jean.'

'Don't be. And we'll make a pact. We may find Herbert or we may not, but let's agree it was worth looking for him.'

They turned round and retraced their steps. The old axiom that turning back appeared to double the distance already walked had never seemed more true, yet Jean felt an enormous relief that the decision had been made. I've never made a better one, she thought. It was strange to see for the first time the exodus of soldiers and refugees coming *towards* them. The new perspective revealed more starkly than ever the dire condition of those on the road. Of course she and Jyoti were the only people walking back towards Tamu.

After a couple of hours, with the light beginning to fail, the increasingly rocky terrain signalled that their target was near. There was no mistaking the rock they'd rested on two hours earlier and Jyoti ran towards it. She turned back to Jean with an anguished expression.

'He's not here. That's where I put him down.'

'Just a minute.' Jean went round to check at the back. The bear was on the ground, lying where he'd landed after toppling off. Jean knelt and slowly poked Herbert's head above the rock surface.

'Hello Jyoti,' she said in a bear-like voice.

Jyoti's face was a crazy mixture of emotions. She plunged forward and hurled herself into Jean's arms. Jean had never heard the girl cry before and the outpouring of heartfelt, squeaky little noises overwhelmed her.

'You cry, darling,' she said, stroking Jyoti's head. 'You cry and cry.'

Jyoti raised her face and burst out 'Will you be my mummy?'

'Oh my dear — I'd like to be,' Jean told her. 'How I'd love to be. But that's something we'll have to talk about.'

She stood with Jyoti's face on her breast, stroking her hair, feeling the impact of the girl's racking sobs. In the background a large company of British soldiers went past in the last extremes of physical disintegration. Some would not go much further. Their eyes stared in hollow sockets. Their legs beneath the shorts were running with open sores. Shirts were black with sweat. They wore useless boots, soles flapping against the uppers, or went barefoot. Jean saw a soldier fall asleep standing up and another walking into a tree. Dysentery was rife and men stopped at the side of the road to shit and were hauled to their feet again by a mate, for the consequences of falling behind were pitiless.

'You cry, darling,' she said again. 'Cry for all of us.'


## ~ Ten ~
### Dimapur rail-head


Nothing about the journey out of Burma was easy, but after Jean and Jyoti went back for Herbert they felt their luck may have changed. They did the next 25 miles from Palel to Imphal in two days of relatively easy walking, on a stretch of road that was in better shape than any they'd used before. Imphal, capital of Manipur state, was on a fertile plateau some two thousand feet high. Here they found another Tea Association camp, the largest they seen, with tents, plenty of rations, and doctors. The man in charge was a friend of Jan's and mention of the Dutchman's name brought an invitation to an evening meal of guinea fowl. It was the best food they'd eaten since leaving Yenangyaung, almost too rich for stomachs used to a scratch diet.

A decent meal was just the start of it. That night they slept under canvas and next morning emerged to find a lorry parked on the road, taking refugees on board. A lorry! It was hard for them to get their heads round the notion that walking was at an end.

Boarding the lorry was not straightforward. The policy laid down was 'women and children first', but the two young soldiers in charge struggled to impose it upon refugees milling around the vehicle. Some of the men had to be physically restrained from thrusting themselves on board first, including a Bengali who was willing to leave his own wife behind. It was a further demonstration of what Jean had observed many times before, that on the trail kindness and selfishness went hand-in-hand. The evening before, their host had described how a gang of Sikhs had to be stopped from commandeering the Tea Association's free food and selling it off to fellow refugees.

When the lorry set off, one of the young soldiers moved inside to keep order, and because Jean was English (and because he took a liking to Jyoti) he fixed them a good spot at the tailgate and stayed there to talk.

Jean sat watching the ground being consumed beneath the lorry's wheels. 'You can't imagine how wonderful this seems,' she told the man, 'After covering every inch of the track on foot. Thank god for the army.'

He laughed. 'Glad to be of service, lady. We come up here with food supplies, then take you people on board going back. You know, the army had 90 of these lorries originally – must be down to 80 now.'

'How come?'

'Oh, a lot of them were nicked from lease-lend stores – US stuff intended for China. We got the lorries but not the spares. The Chinks have it worse – they'll have spares and no lorries. But that's not all. Look out there.'

On one side of the road was a ravine plunging several hundred feet down. Jean looked where the soldier was pointing and saw the carcass of a broken-up lorry at the bottom. It was perhaps as well that most of the refugees couldn't see this, because the lorry resounded with 'oohs' and 'aahs' every time it went over a bump in the road.

'Blimey! What happened down there?' Jean asked.

The soldier shrugged. 'That's not the only one. Some of these young tearaways aren't used to driving this sort of terrain. Actually they're not used to driving lorries full stop. Oh don't worry – you're all right with George.' He nodded towards his mate at the wheel. 'He's pretty safe when sober.'

'So you think we might get there in one piece?' she said.

'Fingers crossed.'

'Get where, incidentally. How far can you take us?'

'All the way, lady. The Dimapur railhead. From there they've got trains across the Bhrahmaputra through Assam. Then for some of these people' – he indicated the crush of Indian refugees in the lorry – 'Back to their homes in Calcutta.'

She thought of Bruce, because he'd left her an address in Calcutta.

'What happens to Indians who've only ever lived in Burma?' she asked.

'They've set up camps for them,' he replied. 'It's all being taken care of.'

In no time at all the lorry pulled up at the Dimapur railhead. Before passengers were allowed out the young soldier made an announcement.

'Listen carefully folks. Dimapur is not a rest camp. The whole idea is to get you people in and out again at speed. When I tell you there are ten trains a day you'll see what I mean. Now the thing is you won't get on one without a ticket from the office here, no way, so the first thing you do – the very first thing – is report there. Off you go then, and good luck.'

The camp's HQ was in a one-storey school building three hundred yards away from the station. Soldiers organised the lorry-load of refugees as they piled into the office area. The first person Jean saw, standing outside talking to an older man, was Bruce. At the same moment he saw her. They stood a few yards apart staring at each other and it was Jyoti who ran up and took him by the hand.

'Hello Jyoti,' he said. 'Where's your mother?'

'She died, Bruce.'

'I'm very sorry to hear that. I'm so sorry.'

Now Jean came forward and shook hands formally. She wanted to cry but restrained herself. 'I'd like to introduce Jean Costain,' Bruce said to the older man. 'Jean, meet Alexander Beattie, the supervisor of this camp. Believe it or not he was manager of a tea estate 50 miles from here.'

'Oh I know all about the Tea Association,' she said, and told Beattie about her meetings with Jan.

'I'm glad you and the young lady got through, Mrs Costain,' Beattie said. 'We should be able to get you on a train soon – maybe tomorrow night?'

'Jean saved my life,' Bruce told him. 'She's a nurse, but she behaves like a doctor.'

'A nurse!' Beattie did a double-take. 'In that case Mrs Costain, can we say a train in three or four days time? If you don't mind.'

She laughed. 'I don't mind. Interesting system you have here.'

'Sorry about that.' Beattie didn't look very sorry. 'I have to take what I can get. That's how I got landed with this man. Found him in a hospital bed but turns out he's a first class organiser.' He began to move off. 'Please Mrs Costain, make sure you come and find me as soon as you feel strong enough for the hospital.'

'There goes a truly amazing man,' Bruce murmured, nodding at Beattie's departing figure.

'Maybe, but he's overdoing things,' Jean said.

Bruce raised his eyebrows. 'So you noticed that. Just what kind of nurse are you?'

'An observant nurse?'

Bruce reached out and took Jyoti's hand. Everything he did was just right for Jean. 'You realise I did have another reason for hanging around here, apart from what he said about organising. I thought sooner or later you'd turn up.'

'And there I was thinking you were in Calcutta.'

'I'm glad to have been in your thoughts at all.'

'Oh yes, you were there.'

A second wave of newcomers brushed noisily past, and they drew reluctantly apart. Camp life was not designed for conducting relationships. Soon after mid-day Jean reported to Beattie. She knew from the way he'd made his request, and the fact he made it at all, that he was desperate for experienced hospital staff. She was happy to work there and 'give something back'. Despite the rigours of the journey she felt good. She *looked* strange, having lost over a stone in weight and with the usual fungal complaints on her skin, but there was strength in her legs and her mind was buzzing as never before. She felt even better after taking a makeshift shower (with Jyoti smuggled in beside her) that was a privilege of working for the hospital. The sensation of being clean all over and strutting about in a new hospital uniform – well, a second-hand one washed and ironed – raised her spirits further.

She worked six hours that day, then laid her ground sheet down in a place Bruce knew of, away from the overpowering stench of excrement, and fell immediately asleep. On the second day she did eight hours, her old stint at the Rangoon hospital. Beattie was doubly glad of her contribution because the day they left Imphal the Japanese bombed the place, and casualties were being ferried down the road to Dimapur. On the second evening Bruce showed her and Jyoti round the camp. She was glad of the two hours they were together. She wanted to spend time with him. She wanted to know that what she felt for him wasn't a schoolgirl passion born of extraordinary circumstances, but something real.

The more she learnt about the camp the more her admiration for Beattie grew. By talking to people and piecing together the evidence of her own eyes, she began to understand the extent of his achievement. Through ability and grindingly hard work and the help of a planter's wife (not his own), he'd developed a nothing site into an outfit that had serviced 32,000 refugees in April alone. Without Beattie a lot more people would have died. His actions affected every element of the camp. He'd had two tube wells sunk and built four 400-gallon water tanks. Hundreds of labourers were recruited from the surrounding areas and put to profitable work. He'd secured a great deal of food in a region where food was scarce and stored it safely (in every room of the school building except the office). Around the school other premises had sprung up constructed from bamboo, with bamboo matting on the ground. There were actually *two* hospitals, both open at the sides – the camp hospital proper, and the Tea Association hospital where Jean worked, a superior operation with better access to drugs. Another bamboo structure housed a canteen for Europeans, a place Jean avoided because of Jyoti. All this activity demanded an array of labourers, managers, clerks, interpreters, doctors, nurses and engineers, hand-picked and closely monitored by Beattie himself.

Meanwhile the planter's wife, with the help of her own servants, had constructed cooking stoves and collected an arsenal of utensils, made bread, and grown vegetables, all for a massive catering operation conducted in the most unpropitious of circumstances.

On her third evening in Dimapur Jean was invited to join Beattie for dinner. This, the equivalent of a royal summons, could not be ignored, and in any case Beattie said he had two pieces of information to convey. And he wanted to pick her brains about the hospital. 'He does that,' said Bruce, who'd offered to look after Jyoti while Jean was occupied.

She and the supervisor sat in a corner of the canteen away from the handful of other customers. The place was lit by oil lamps that attracted dozens of insects. The canteen staff pressed around Beattie, attentive to his every whim, though he was the last man to demand special attention. The two of them were brought soup, then chicken and rice. As they ate she tentatively relayed some thoughts about the work – how to rationalise the two hospitals, manage the drug supply, adjust the distribution of patient beds.

'They're just thoughts,' she said. 'Other people will know better.'

After the meal they drank tea. 'I told you I had some news for you, Mrs Costain,' Beattie said. 'It's about your husband.'

She went red. 'Oh! About Philip?'

He nodded. 'It's all right, he's alive, if that's what you're thinking about. He was here you know, in the hospital.'

'I didn't know.' She was trying to drag her thoughts round to Philip from someone else. She didn't like herself at such moments.

'Sorry it's taken me so long to tell you. I thought I remembered him...had to check our records. His jaw had been smashed by a bullet. It's a serious injury but he should be all right. Bruce doesn't know about this by the way.'

'I see.' Beattie seemed able to guess what she was thinking before she knew it herself. 'Where *is* Philip?' she asked.

'That's what I needed to check. As you know, we don't hold on to the serious cases here. He was taken to the Baptist Mission Hospital in Gauhati. I've just managed to make contact with them. He's still there. Seems to be progressing well.'

She began to speak but he was ahead of her again. 'We're transferring another two patients to Gauhati tomorrow. You could go with them if you like – in fact it would help us if you did. Take your girl with you.'

'Thank you Mr Beattie. And thank you for taking all this trouble.'

'Actually it's I who am in your debt,' Beattie went on. 'You've been a big help to us. Bruce said you knew what you were doing. Quite apart from hard work, you have a way of thinking laterally. It's unusual.'

'Do you think so?'

'I don't mind telling you, Mrs Costain, I'd move heaven and earth to hold on to you, but for one thing.'

'You mean Jyoti?' she said.

He nodded. 'This is no place for someone her age. You know, very few children make it through the sort of journey you've done. She must be quite a girl.'

'There's no-one like her,' said Jean.

'Working here for these few months,' he said, 'You get an insight into who survives and why. I believe you were just a group of three?'

'Just me, Jyoti, and Jyoti's mother.'

'Hmm. Most people have travelled in larger numbers. Then group dynamics play a part. Leaders are important, of course. And cooks. Decent food is a big morale boost.'

'Jyoti's mother was a wonderful cook,' Jean said.

Beattie grunted, and she wasn't sure he'd heard. The supervisor had retreated into his own thoughts, scarcely aware of her presence. 'On the whole women have been more resourceful than the men,' he mused. 'The effects of age are less predictable. Older men do as well as young ones. Babies often survive, surprisingly.' He sipped the dregs of his tea, oblivious to the fact that they were cold. 'We've seen such heartache here. Families in disarray. The weak left behind to make their own way. For many of them Dimapur was the end of the line, not the beginning. They'd get this far with nothing left, hear the clang of the shunting trucks, and let go. Our cemetery is full of them.'

The canteen was empty except for the table they sat at. Staff stood by in a group waiting patiently for their supervisor to finish. The humidity was more oppressive than Jean would ever have thought possible. She was wet all over, and Beattie's crumbling features dripped sweat from every crevice. Outside came the sound of a high wind crashing through palm trees.

'Do you think we should leave, Mr Beattie?' she asked.

Suddenly he was back with her, out of his reverie. 'Now then Mrs Costain.' He stressed the name like a man confirming her identity. 'There's something else I must tell you – or rather, ask you. I've been requested to do so by Her Majesty's government in London. You know about gongs, I suppose?'

She looked at him stupidly. An image of the gong in J. Arthur Rank films went through her head.

'You've been put up for an MBE,' Beattie went on. 'Bruce Scott is the culprit. The way these things work, I ask if you're willing to accept it. Are you?'

Jean sat open-mouthed. She remembered Scott saying 'Thank you for your help', and remarking 'It won't be forgotten, I promise'.

'Mrs Costain?' Beattie pressed.

'I...I'm not worth that,' she stammered.

'Now don't you go turning it down,' he said. 'You'd have every nurse in the forces on your back.'

'I suppose so.' She was utterly dazed. 'All right, thank you.'

'That's it then. I'll report back to them. Well, I suppose we ought to be going.' He began to stand, then sat down heavily. 'Just a minute...'

'Mr Beattie,' she said. 'Are you all right?'

'I will be. Give me a moment.'

He wasn't a man whose manner encouraged personal observations – certainly not from a young whipper-snapper like herself – but she made up her mind to say something. 'Mr Beattie, I *am* a nurse after all. Don't you think...I mean, wouldn't it be an idea for you to take a few weeks off. Have a rest and come back refreshed. You've done so much.' He stared at her. 'I'm sorry, Mr Beattie, but somebody had to say that.'

She thought he was angry but Beattie gave a wry smile. 'It's all right Mrs Costain, I don't bite. The point is, sometimes we find our metier by accident, don't you think. You would know that, of all people.'

'I don't understand.'

'No. Tell me, do you think tea is exciting?'

'Tea?' She laughed. 'I like a nice cup of tea.'

'I did it for 30 years on my plantation. Then this work came along by accident. Nothing I've ever done compares. I'm content for it to see me out.'

When Jean left the canteen, Bruce was waiting in the shelter with Jyoti. He ruffled the girl's hair. 'Thought she'd be drier in here,' he said. 'The monsoon's about to break.'

She told them about the next day's visit to Philip in Gauhati.

'In that case may I invite you to come for a stroll,' Bruce said, moving outside and beckoning.

'A stroll! Are you crazy. Jyoti and I have to...'

She broke off as Jyoti pushed her out of the shelter with an elegant gesture reminiscent of her mother. 'See you later Jean,' the girl called, shooing her away.

They went at random round the camp environs, scarcely noticing where their feet led. They walked past the water towers down to the track, where the 10pm train – last of the day – was getting up steam and soldiers shepherded refugees to the carriages in more or less orderly fashion. The whole camp was congested with Indians, standing or sitting in groups, several thousand people awaiting their turn on the trains the next day. There was a frenetic atmosphere, a heightened sense of expectancy in the ridiculous heat and humidity as the rain clouds threatened to break.

Jean walked close to Bruce, her shoulder touching his. She was caught up in the mood of the evening, the feeling of suspense. She was on a precipice ready to jump, wanting to tell him everything.

'I'm in a state about tomorrow,' she said. 'What I'm going to find, what I should say. I owe him something – I'm his wife after all. I ought to be concerned about him but...you know, I've hardly given Philip a thought in weeks. I want you to understand what a self-centred little bitch I am.'

Most men might have said something in reply but Bruce seemed to understand that silence would bring more.

'My life was all mapped out in Rangoon,' she went on. 'Everything was settled from the beginning, and not by me. Then in just three months out here...the thing is, I didn't know. I didn't know who I was.'

'The war,' he said, the very parody of a laconic Englishman.

She said 'If two words are all I'm going to get, there are some things I want to tell you.'

'You don't need to say anything.'

'No, but I want to. When we were in Prome, we couldn't get a boat. We were stuck there for days. To get us onto one I offered the captain a service. I thought he'd go for a white woman, even a bony creature like me.'

Bruce took her hand and squeezed it.

'Then I met a Dutch planter on that boat, and again when we walked through Tamu.' Everything was pouring out now; she couldn't have stopped. 'He really likes me and I like him. But that's not what I want because all the time I've been thinking about you. I love you, that's what, I love you, and god I feel so much better for saying it, and I think I *can* say it because I've never understood before and now I do, if the word has any meaning at all. I'm a married woman and...and I believe if I were free that you might care for me, if you weren't so proper and honourable and bloody monosyllabic.'

In a tacit search for more privacy they colluded to find the camp cemetery, the one place free from refugees. It was a sad spot under palm trees, row after row of crude wooden crosses signifying the numbers who'd died at the railhead, 'hearing the clang of the shunting trucks'. Bruce came to a halt there and spread his arms in mock outrage.

'Monosyllabic! I keep telling you I think you're great.'

'*Keep* telling me!' she cried. 'You said it once a month ago and don't think I didn't notice.'

A tremendous sheet of lightning came down, illuminating every detail of the cemetery as if it were under arc lights. Seconds later thunder broke like an air attack. In no time the rain had drenched them both, and in howling wind the palm trees bent to insane angles.

'Come out from under the trees,' Bruce shouted over the noise, pulling her by the arm. 'It's dangerous.'

'And suppose I don't want to,' she cried, pulling back.

The sodden dress was clinging to every line of her meagre body. Her took her in both arms and kissed her until she kissed him back and went on kissing him. She felt his own body respond, and as the knot in his thighs pressed against her something happened that had never occurred, *never*, in all her time with Philip, and she wondered if Bruce had noticed and thought he would have because her lips had gone slack.

As they walked back to the shelter to get Jyoti she asked him 'Do you like children?'

'That's like asking "Do you like people?"' he said. 'I can think of one child who is a delight to be with.'

'I know.' She looked suddenly grim. 'I have to go and talk to her mother's sister. I'm dreading it. They'll want to take her back. My life is such a mess.'

'I shall want to know how much of a mess,' he said, 'Every step of the way.'

She turned to him. 'In that case I shall keep you informed.'

They found a dry Jyoti under the shelter. The girl goggled at their saturated clothes. 'I like to see people enjoying themselves,' she said, wearing her most cheeky expression. 'Is it the true expression, Jean, to say "drowned rats"?'

'You mean, is it the *correct* expression,' Jean replied primly.

## ~ Eleven ~
## Into India

Jean set off for Gauhati at 9am the following morning. She stayed inside the ambulance with the two wounded men and Jyoti sat at the front with the driver. The journey took several hours, but everything seemed easy now they weren't foot-slogging. And caring for a couple of casualties was a doddle compared to two lorry-loads of Scott's wounded men.

Gauhati was located between the banks of the Bhramaputra river and the foothills of the Shillong plateau. She'd not been there before despite her many India years, but knew it was considered the largest and most metropolitan town in Assam – hence the above-average medical facilities.

When they arrived, porters emerged from the hospital with stretchers, and she oversaw the transfer of the wounded men into the building. The Matron there was an agreeable middle-aged woman who immediately laid on cups of tea. Jean described the circumstances that had led to Jyoti and her ending up in Dimapur.

'What a time you must have had,' the woman said, openly appraising them. 'Tell me, if you were in the Rangoon hospital you must have worked under Peggy.'

'You know her?' Jean asked.

'Oh we go back a long way. We trained together at Lady Minto's

Nursing Association in Calcutta. Centuries ago.' The Matron gave a mischievous grin. 'I think Peggy could be described as a character.'

'She was very good to me though she pretended not to be,' Jean said. 'Have you heard if she's all right – now the Japanese are in Rangoon?'

'I did get news from someone who knows her. I gather she's giving the invaders a hard time.'

'No surprise there then. Forgive me Matron, but I had an ulterior motive for wanting to be here today. I believe you have a captain Philip Costain as a patient.'

The woman gave an old-fashioned look. 'There's nobody of that rank here.'

'Pardon me?'

'Just kidding,' the Matron said. 'It's *Major* Costain now. And if I'm not mistaken, you'll be his wife. He's in ward 3. Go on up. I'll look after this young woman for you.'

Patrick was in a room with half-a-dozen other men and a strong smell of disinfectant. She'd not told him she was coming and for a split second neither of them was sure of the other's identity. Jean had lost a lot of weight from a frame that couldn't afford it, and he was showing the effects of his injury. His face, rearranged by the bullet, had a lop-sided look under its supporting wiring. The bustling confidence he'd always conveyed had given way to an air of fragility. He looked older.

'Jean? Is it really you?'

'How are you Philip? I'm sorry you had to go through this.'

'It's all right. I'm one of the lucky ones.'

'I believe congratulations are in order.'

'Oh that. A mixed blessing. Promotions come faster during a war.'

'But I did say you were promotion material, remember.'

He told her what had happened since Yenangyaung, and she gave an account of her travels. He didn't actually express regret at Deepa's death but commented 'That journey was always a tough ask'.

'I have Jyoti here with me,' she said.

'Jyoti?'

'The daughter. I'm taking her to Deepa's sister today but I don't want to. I don't want to let her go.'

He looked up sharply, wincing at the effort. 'What do you mean?'

'What I'd really like is to adopt her.'

'Adopt an *Indian* girl!'

'That's right.'

She *wanted* this kind of reaction from him; wanted ammunition for her decision, which would not wear well even in her eyes. Women were supposed to be loyal to army spouses, especially in wartime.

'Are you going to be all right?' she asked.

'I'll heal. Should have a more interesting face at the end of it. I may have to give up eating steak though.' He pulled himself up in the bed. 'You don't need to worry, Jean. You won't be abandoning an old crock.'

It was said kindly, not to score points. He was making things easy for her; in fact he'd foretold their future before she had. The man still had the capacity to surprise.

'The trouble is I can't change,' he said. 'I'm a straight up and down army bloke. Always will be.'

'I know. I'm sorry. I think I *am* different. All sorts of stuff has happened. I can't even talk about some of it.'

'You could hardly go through all that and not change,' he said. 'You've been brilliant, Jean. I didn't give you a cat's chance in hell but you pulled it off. I take my hat off to you.'

'Oh Philip.'

His being nice to her wasn't part of the plan. She felt tears pricking her eyelids – again – and thought 'What a soggy apology for a woman I am.'

'You do realise it won't be easy,' he went on. 'You know what people are like about divorce.'

The room had gone quiet as the other patients listened in. She wondered how a marriage could end so sedately, with regret but no great pain. Everything they owned was ransacked in Rangoon, so no possessions to be divvied up, not even a child. There was just the unspoken censure of Philip's colleagues and her own self-deprecation.

'I suppose you'd better leave,' Philip said into the pregnant silence. 'We don't want to get maudlin.'

She got obediently to her feet and leaned down for a kiss, avoiding the lower half of his face.

'Drop me a line now and then,' he said. 'I'd like to know how you get on.'

'And make sure you reply,' she responded.

If the first part of the day was easier than anticipated, the rest of it was hell. Deepa's sister lived in Shillong, some 40 miles south of Gauhati in the Khasia Hills. Jean had sent the woman a telegram – about Deepa's death and Jyoti's future – and didn't know if it had been received. But while they were so near Shillong she thought it would be daft not to go.

The first step was to consult the authorities. Gauhati housed the main centre for the British administration in Assam, and Jean asked the Dimapur driver to drop them off there. She was advised that the man in charge could see her in 20 minutes.

In the sober waiting room, on uncomfortable wooden chairs, she tried to explain her position to Jyoti. 'I want you to understand that the thing I would most like is for you to stay with me. Not Philip, by the way – just you and me, and maybe one other, if he'll have me. I love you, Jyoti, I love you so much and it would make me happy.' The words echoed in the empty room and she lowered her voice. 'But we *must* talk to your mother's sister and find out what she wants. She's your family, your flesh and blood, and she'll have the law on her side if she wants you with her. Do you see?'

'It's all right Jean. I understand.'

The girl had reverted to the introspective mood Jean remembered from their first few meetings, civil but unforthcoming. The defence mechanism was understandable. Jean sensed it in her own mood, her preparation for loss. She felt as if something was being torn away from her body.

The British official was amiable and helpful. He thought a visit to Shillong would be sensible, especially from the legal angle. And to her surprise he offered one of their chauffeur-driven cars to take them there.

The driver was a tiny local man who spoke good English. 'Thank you for taking us to Shillong,' she told him.

'Nice drive for me, madam,' was all he offered in reply. Otherwise little was said on the 90-minute drive. They climbed several thousand feet into the hills and the heat fell away.

'At least it would be nice and cool living up here,' Jean said with an attempt at brightness, but Jyoti barely responded. 'I know, Jyoti,' she went on, 'But we have to see them. They're your blood family and I'm not. I wish I were.'

'I wish you were too,' Jyoti said.

Entering Shillong itself, Jean observed that there were no old buildings. 'Earthquake, madam,' the driver interpolated 'Year 1897. Whole town knocked down. New houses come up.'

All too soon they arrived at their destination. The driver pulled up by a small concrete house in a nondescript street.

'This is the place, madam.'

A woman opened the door in response to their knock. Jean surmised that she'd have been a few years older than Deepa. The telegram had been received and she knew Jean's name. She kissed Jyoti, who received her embrace like a block of stone.

'I'm Uma,' the woman said, ushering them into the living room. She introduced her husband and two young daughters, who stood stiffly by as if participating in a group photograph.

Uma went into the kitchen to make tea. Her husband ignored Jean and talked in Hindi to Jyoti, who responded in the manner of a prisoner in the dock. The daughters were staring at Jyoti with barely disguised hostility. Perched awkwardly on the edge of the sofa, Jean became aware of an undercurrent that she was quite unable to interpret. It occurred to her that she'd never before been isolated in an Indian household, which said a lot about her and the British and the Raj.

Uma returned and the adults drank tea. There was some talk about

Deepa, and Jean described the last tragic days of her life. The husband contributed briefly in English which, it turned out, he spoke quite well. Uma's comments were distinctly restrained and Jean began to wonder how well the sisters had got on.

After twenty minutes the atmosphere showed no signs of warming up. I could sit here for hours and nothing would change, Jean thought; time for my prepared speech.

'I wanted to come and see you,' she began, 'Because of Jyoti's future.' She told them she knew they were Jyoti's flesh and blood and cared what happened to her; what she didn't know was whether they could consider an addition to their family. Every word she said sounded wooden and patronising and likely to cause offence.

'There's one more thing I want to say,' she ended up. 'In the past few months Jyoti and I have been through a lot together and I have come to love her as if she was my own child. If you did not object I would very much like to look after her myself, to adopt her into my own family. Of course if that happened I would keep you fully informed about her future life.'

The room was silent after she'd said this little piece. Everything about the scene seemed unnatural, as if they were characters in a badly performed play. Jyoti had scarcely moved since the moment they arrived.

The husband and wife exchanged a few words in Hindi. 'We want to thank you for looking after the girl,' the wife said eventually. 'But of course Jyoti is part of our family and it is for us to give her a home. We thank you again for all your help.'

There were more platitudes but Jean couldn't take them in because she was feeling sick.  After a bit she realised the family were expecting her to leave, so got to her feet.  She'd known it could come to this but was still unprepared.  She told Jyoti she would write and come back to see her, and kissed the frozen face.  Without wanting to she found herself standing on the doorstep, then walking out towards the car.  By the time she'd turned back to wave, the door had closed.

The driver turned the ignition and Jean climbed into the passenger seat.  The man looked enquiringly and she spread her hands in a gesture of helplessness.  Too stupefied to cry, for once, she had a dozen different thoughts running through her head, the worst of them contemplating Jyoti sold into slavery.  She knew it could happen; this was India.

The driver took the car 50 yards down the road and stopped, turning off the ignition.

'What are you doing?' Jean said in a distraught, squeaky little voice.

'Wait a moment, madam,' he said.  'Be calm.'

Hearing a door slam, then footsteps, she got out of the car.  Jyoti was charging down the road towards her, not just running but leaping about and grinning all over her face.  She bounded up to Jean, gave her a big hug, and let loose an enormous cry of 'Whoopee!'.

'What the devil...what's going on?' Jean cried, completely disoriented.  'Didn't they want you to stay?'

Jyoti was chortling gleefully.  'Three daughters in one family, Jean? *I don't think so*!  We're talking three lots of dowry, you know.'

'But then...'  She still couldn't get her head round it.  'Why on earth didn't they say so?'

'Not Indian way, madam.'  The little driver was out of the car, grinning. 'Not wanting to lose face.'

'Now look here, Jyoti.' Jean stared at the girl suspiciously. 'Look at you now, laughing and leaping about like a cat with two tails. In there, in their house, you were a little iceberg.'

'I am Indian girl, Jean, with many tails. Indian girl must be very tricky. Have to make bad impression so family don't want me.'

Jean regarded the prancing figure with new eyes. 'Why, you crafty little minx. I see I shall have to keep a very close watch on you.'

'You should. I am girl growing up, soon to be teenager. This is the time when we girls become difficult.'

Jean pointed to the back seat. 'Get in the car.'

Jyoti saluted. 'Yes, *sir.*'

When all three of them were in, the driver asked 'Where to, madam?'

'Away from Shillong as fast as possible. Let's go back to Gauhati.' She touched his arm. 'And thank you.'

'No problem, madam.'

As they reached the centre of Gauhati Jean said 'You know what, Jyoti, I think we should celebrate.' She turned to the driver. 'Could you stop here please.'

She thanked him again and handed over a large tip. They got out in the busy shopping centre, opposite an ice-cream parlour. In the road, traffic roared past. It was hard to imagine that a war was raging a couple of hundred miles south.

'Come on,' Jean said.

She was surprised to see an ice-cream parlour operating in Assam, but the place was open all right and quite well patronised, perhaps partly because it was so cool inside. They sat on high stools that gave them a view out of the window.

'Do you know what an ice-cream sundae is?' Jean asked.

'I don't think so, Jean.'

'It's ice cream with extra stuff, like cream and fruit. Would you like to try one?'

'Gosh, I would.'

A waiter materialised and told them about flavours.

'So what will you have then?' Jean asked.

'Well, not vanilla,' Jyoti said. 'Either strawberry or chocolate. Oh it's so difficult.'

'Make up your mind.'

'Strawberry then. Can I have that?'

The ice-creams arrived and Jyoti demolished hers in a matter of minutes. She sat watching while Jean finished her vanilla sundae in a more ladylike manner.

'Do you think, Jean...' she began.

'What now?'

'Well, I was wondering...do you think I could have a chocolate one as well?'

Jean swivelled round on the stool. 'Now look Jyoti, we're going to be together for good from now on, so I shall have to start behaving like a proper mother. And proper mothers don't let their daughter have everything they want, do they?'

'No. Sorry, Jean.'

'I've already said — I shall have to keep an eye on you now I've discovered how crafty you are.'

'Yes Jean, you're right.'

They sat staring out of the window at the scooters and rickshaws going past.  Here in the cool ice-cream parlour it was hard to credit all they'd been through in the preceding months.  The Kabaw Valley seemed like a bad dream.

Jean gave a furtive sideways glance and found Jyoti staring demurely up at her.  'Oh, for goodness sake.'  Jean beckoned to the waiter.  'A chocolate sundae, please.'  To Jyoti she said 'And that's all you're getting, so make the most of it.'

'Of course, Jean.  Thank you, Jean.'

## ~ A note on sources ~

I was one year old in 1942 and have never been to Burma, so I needed to lean heavily on the published literature for background material on the military retreat and the exodus of civilians.

*Military*
James Lunt. *A hell of a licking: the retreat from Burma 1941-2*. Collins, 1986.
My bible on military matters. An account of the British army's retreat by someone who was there. A careful and very readable historical record with interesting judgements of people and events. Includes an invaluable selective bibliography.

Tim Carew. *The longest retreat*. Hamish Hamilton, 1969.
An uneven, gung-ho, colourfully written popular history concentrating on personalities. Bizarre collection of photographs.

Tony Mains. *The retreat from Burma*. Foulsham, 1973.
Sober account by an intelligence officer who was one of the 'last-ditchers' in Rangoon. Good on Burmese communications in 1942.

Jon Latimer. *Burma: the forgotten war*. Murray, 2004.
Scissors and paste job. Some telling details culled from other sources, confusingly presented.

John A Baty. *Surgeon in the jungle war*. Kimber, 1979.
Good on various medical details – war wounds, diseases, jungle infections.

Julian Thompson. *Forgotten voices of Burma*. Ebury Press, 2009.
Records testimony from all ranks about the more human aspects of war. The three entries by the military wife, Mrs Margaret Bootland, were the inspiration for writing this novel.

*The civilian exodus*
Hugh Tinker. A forgotten long march: The Indian exodus from Burma
1942. *Journal of South-east Asian studies* Vol VI, no. 1 March 1975.
Informative academic article on the Indian exodus. Especially good on
official initiatives (or lack of them).

Marjorie C Nickerson. *Burma interlude*. Topgallant Publishing
(Honolulu), 1981.
A military wife describes her escape from central Burma into India via
the Kalewa route, travelling by paddle-steamer and on foot.

Francis Clifford. *Desperate journey*. Hodder & Stoughton, 1979.
Compelling narrative by Arthur Thompson (aka the novelist, Francis
Clifford) who led a small group of soldiers out of Burma by the
'impossible' Fort Hertz route.

Geoffrey Tyson. *Forgotten frontier*. W H Tartett & Co. (Calcutta), 1945.
A surprise treasure of a book, describing help given by planters from the
Indian Tea Association to refugees exiting Burma by various routes.
Very well put together and – a rarity – contains some excellent
photographs.

E V C Foucar. *I lived in Burma*. Dennis Dobson, 1956.
Superficial observations of a British citizen who lived in Burma for 40
years. When war came he escaped via the Kalewa route.


*Other*
Alistair McCrae & Alan Prentice. *Irrawaddy flotilla*. James Paton Ltd,
1978.
Well-researched and well-written history of the company that ran
paddle-steams on Burma's rivers. An excellent chapter on the war
years.

George Rodger. *Red moon rising*. Cresset Press, 1943.
Observant report by an American war photographer who travelled
widely in Burma during 1942. Many first-rate photographs.

Alfred Wagg. *A million died: A story of war in the far east*. Nicolson & Watson, 1943.
Muddled, vainglorious account – mostly hearsay – by an American war correspondent. Best chapter is a graphic report on the battle of Yenangyaung by Darrell Berrigan.

Mi Mi Khaing. *Burmese family*. Longmans, 1946.
A much-needed local perspective by a young Burmese woman on life in her country up to 1941. Many appealing details.

*V.Gorman*

I read it in a short time as I was captivated by the story. *Andywal*

A totally compelling read. *Autopilot*

Well written and absorbing. *Mr P M Coxall*

I have a soft spot for this book. Brilliant story line and exciting all the while. *The lodger*

This is an interesting and quite different storyline which is also well researched. *Citabria*

Made in United States
Orlando, FL
18 April 2024

45905420R00136